Innocence

Gavin Corbett

POCKET BOOKS

TOWNHOUSE

First published in Great Britain and Ireland by Pocket/Townhouse, 2003
An imprint of Simon & Schuster UK Ltd, and
TownHouse Ltd, Dublin

Simon & Schuster UK is a Viacom company

1 3 5 7 9 10 8 6 4 2

Simon & Schuster UK Ltd
Africa House
64–78 Kingsway
London WC2B 6AH

Simon & Schuster Australia
Sydney

TownHouse Ltd
Trinity House
Charleston Road
Ranelagh
Dublin 6
Ireland

A CIP catalogue record for this book is available from the British Library

ISBN 1 903650 29 1

Typeset in Garamond by M Rules
Printed and bound in Great Britain
by Cox & Wyman Ltd, Reading, Berks

Thank you Treasa and all at TownHouse in Dublin for taking the initial leap of faith, and for the hard work and guidance thereafter. Thank you Jane and all at Simon and Schuster in London for editorial expertise. Thank you Mum, Dad, Ciara, Orla, Ronan and Colin for support through the years. Thank you Jennifer for encouraging me to write in the first place, and for a very happy last six years. Thank you Joanne for the Irish-language translations. And thanks to colleagues and the odd friend.

For Jennifer

1

ONE

. . . Cancer, cancer . . .

If you say it enough times you'll get it.

It's like those people who imagine piranhas or Pac-men coursing through their systems eating up malignant cells thinking it'll cure them. Mind over matter sort of thing. Well the reverse is probably true too.

I've known three people in my life with cancer. The first was Ultan Collins' little brother Fiachra, who got leukaemia when he was eight. I felt guilty when he got sick because Ultan and myself used to tease the poor little shit about his weight problem. Nothing malicious, like, just names and things. The funny thing was the chemo made him look even fatter because he lost all his hair and ended up with this big moon face, like a bowling ball with the finger-holds and shit. You could see up his nostrils, but that was just the way his nose was anyway, all stumpy. I stopped eating chips and Brunches for a year just with the thought. Ultan said the steroids made him puff out a lot too before he really began to lose the pounds.

Anyway, he died, but there was this girl I got to know in the same ward as Fiachra who was a bit older than me. I was fourteen at the time and she was seventeen I think. Lorraine was her name. I got talking to her through visiting Fiachra with Ultan. We didn't live too far from the hospital and after a while I found myself going on my own just to visit Lorraine. She was great with Fiachra because she used to slag him in a friendly way that made him laugh. I learned a lot about slagging people from her. She was like a mother and a really sound sister at the same time. She'd call Fiachra her little snotser. I tried using her style and started calling Fiachra 'fatser' but it didn't work as well.

Lorraine didn't wear pyjamas or night dresses like the other patients. She'd have these baggy T-shirts with her favourite bands printed on them. If I had to fault her it was her taste in music. She'd give me these tapes but I wasn't having any of it. It's not my sort of thing at all that. All those whiny bands who'd go around going, '*Uuugh there's no hope, uuugh. I just wanna die, I think I'll slit my wrists. Kill me please. Uuugh. Uuuuuuuuuuuugh.*' I know I shouldn't laugh now, but it was grand; she didn't mind me taking the piss.

I saw her scar once. I didn't want to see it at first because I thought it'd be oozing and freaky but she insisted that it wasn't so bad. She lifted the side of her T-shirt and showed me the stitching going up her side and she was right. It wasn't so disgusting. All scabby, like, but straight, clean, nothing you couldn't deal with. She needed an operation, not like Fiachra, who had the cancer right through his blood. Hers started with a tumour which had to be removed. She once showed me this kiwi fruit from a bowl beside her bed and told me the lump was as big as that. I read about this American woman in a magazine who had a tumour in her belly as big as a water melon and she survived. Lorraine's tumour was only as big as a *kiwi*. She didn't have to lose her hair which was nice because it was red in that all-right way which didn't attract any freckles to her face.

I felt more sorry for her parents than I did for Lorraine. At least she was happy-go-lucky. I could see that her parents used to embarrass her and sometimes annoy her. Getting embarrassed or annoyed put colour back in her cheeks. Her parents were always looking for their value for money out of the nurses so Lorraine would get the best attention. Lorraine kept on telling them to stop making such a big fuss.

'The pain killers are part of the service, pet. Don't be afraid to ask for them.' All this shit, right in front of the nurse.

'Just *ask* for tea whenever you want it. It's no skin off their teeth.'

They meant 'nose'. Me and Lorraine used to laugh at that when they were gone because that was one of her Da's favourite sayings. Her Ma used to fluff up her pillows even when she was comfortable. She'd make her sit up for a second and thump the flatness and the body heat out – *phwump, phwump* – and turn it over to the other side. That used to bug the shit out of her she'd tell me. I thought at the time she was going through one of those phases.

The nurses allowed Lorraine's parents to bring her in this puppy once. That was around the time they moved her into a room on her own. She was getting in a bad way. Being isolated made her lonely and upset so her parents got her the puppy to cheer her up. I was there when they brought it in. It was a mongrel. Half a cocker spaniel and something else. She called it Keith. I thought that was really funny calling a dog a human's name. It was a boy's name too and when I got Keith after Lorraine died I checked it and it wasn't even male. That was a nice touch on her parents' part giving me the dog but I'm not really a dog person and I gave it away to a home a couple of weeks later.

The last time I saw Lorraine I'll never forget the screams. She got really bad very suddenly and the worst thing was I'd left visiting her for about ten days. When I came in that time she was wired up more heavily than usual. The wires normally led to bags of salt and glucose and shit, but this time there was this machine. It kept on bleeping beside her and every couple of minutes this older man in a dressing gown who I'd never seen before kept popping into the room like she'd made some new friend or something and kept saying this machine was making a weird noise. But it wasn't a weird noise. It was normal I'm sure. I think he just used to like the sound of his own voice making that word 'weird' string out in a culchie accent. He began to bug the shit out of me. Dickie was his name he told me. One of those names that sticks in your brain. The weird world of Dickie.

I was with her for about an hour and all she did was groan lightly and sort of purr. She was virtually asleep. I didn't really know what to say but I just kept on talking to her. I'm quite good at keeping up a conversation with somebody who doesn't talk back. I find it easier and things flow more easily. There's no pressure. But after a while I saw her lips open as if she was about to say something. They sort of peeled open from left to right because they were so dry.

'Oh, Jesus. Jesus.'

It started off quietly in a husky way, then got louder.

'Jesus Christ. Jesus Fucking Christ.'

I made for the door and then got confused. I ran back to the cabinet beside her bed to ring the bell. Then I realized this was thick because I should have just ran to the nurses' station because it seemed like an emergency and then I realized I shouldn't have left her on her own and should just go for the bell anyway and then this team of nurses arrived.

'Oh Christ. Jesus Fucking Christ help me. Jesus. Help me.'

It really got to me. I'd never heard her sound so serious before. One of the nurses kept on messing around with this needle and dropped it on the floor. When she sprayed a bit of the fluid out to get it to the right measurement it got me in the eye. *Ah! Zing!* I was told to go to the bathroom at once to wash it out.

'At once!' she was going, the nurse, 'at once!'

'Christ almighty. Christ al-fucking-mighty! Jesus Fucking Christ!'

I was sort of rooted to the spot for a minute. I hated the screams but I thought I might be able to help maybe.

'*Jesus Fucking Christ!*'

'Go!' The nurse pointed to the door.

I went out into the corridor and made my way to the visitors' bathroom. The echoing of the screams out there freaked me out more. Everything was smoothed and plastered into rounded corners that soaked up the smell of old disinfectant and puke from a hundred years back and made the screams bounce around like mad. I thought I might be able to wash my eye and then come back in but now I didn't want to go back. Outside it sounded like terror. All this sort of moaning and pathetic whining and just terror.

I remember Lorraine and me had this conversation about all death and shit before. Talk about awkward. I'd been trying to avoid that subject. She never referred to herself but she actually thought it was pretty deadly and glamorous and romantic to die young. Maybe she knew right then and she was trying to convince herself that there was something positive about the whole thing. I don't know. I didn't try to argue with her. I think she was deluded by all those bands she used to listen to. Here's what I think: it's just a shitty mess; full stop.

They're saying mobile phones can give you brain tumours nowadays. I mean, the *papers* are saying this nowadays, not the *phones* are more dangerous nowadays. They're always coming out with shit like that. First it was red food colouring in sweets, then it was coffee, then it was burst ink cartridges in computer printers, then it was something else. Some of it might be true. They're called carcinogens. I'll tell you what were dangerous. When I was really little there were these sweets called Kola Rollers which were covered in this silvery substance you could see your face in. They did these tests on them and found there was real aluminium in the coating. *I* could have told them that. They looked too fake to be good for you. Jesus. When I think about it now. We used to devour those things.

*

Then last year there was my Da. He died last year but he had the cancer for a while before that. The thing was, the doctor told him that the tumour had probably been growing inside for six months, but he only really deteriorated after they took him into hospital. Before that he'd only been suffering slightly, but it was like a bad flu: a rattly cough and the odd ache and pain. He used to smoke like a chimney. He was a forty-a-day man. I'm a twenty-a-day man myself. That's what I inherited from my Da. Impatience and dark hair and double-jointedness at the base of my thumb and a nut allergy and an addiction for nicotine.

It wasn't unusual for him to have a bit of a cough sometimes. As well as being a heavy smoker he worked in a carpet shop where there was always dust flying around, so it never really bothered him that much if he had a tickly throat. He just took it for granted. I suppose he'd been having a bit more hassle than usual for a few weeks before he went to the doctor. His lungs seemed more snotty than normal. He'd cough maybe once or twice a minute and every time he did it sounded like a load of stones being thrown around a biscuit tin. Then he'd have to either swallow or spit out whatever shit had come into his mouth.

This one time when I came home on my lunch I found Da sitting in front of the TV eating a roll or a sandwich. Even before I walked in the gates I could hear him cough from outside. I figured something must have been up: Da never came home for his lunch and I knew for a fact that he took his break at a different time to me. He said he hadn't been feeling too great at work and the lads had told him to take the rest of the day off. He thought he might have picked up some sort of bug. Then he asked me how my day was at school and he started to go on with some bollocks about how I was a good lad and shit. He just wanted to change the subject quickly because he knew I was going to nag him about going to the doctor's.

I went into the kitchen to put on some lunch and then I heard him cough again. But this one wasn't like a short sharp bang bang sort of cough. It went on and wouldn't stop, like a wave, like spasms. He was sort of coughing and choking at the same time. I left the beans on the hob and came back in because I was worried that he was coughing so much he wouldn't get a chance to breathe. He was going on like this for nearly a minute and his face was this red colour. When this stopped he was standing there with his hands on his knees breathing in relief like he'd run a marathon. Then he lifted his right hand to sort of hold his brow. There was this wad of snot all over his trouser leg and it was red and bloody. He didn't say anything, partly because he was knackered and partly because he knew the game was up and he'd have to go to the doctor. I made him promise he'd go by the time I got back from school but I knew he wouldn't and I said that to him too.

I was right as well. He said it was nothing a few Disprins couldn't fix. I sort of got angry then. I told him he was full of shit, plain and simple. There was a bit of a fight.

Something must have happened at work the next day because he went to the doctor straight after. One of the lads must have convinced him in a way I couldn't. Maybe fighting wasn't the way to go about it.

The doctor made him go in for tests almost immediately. That was on the Wednesday. It was amazing because everything happened so quickly. Da said it was funny because the bit of the X-ray where the lump was looked in a better state than the healthy bit. He thought it should have been the other way around. The bad bit was dark and clear and the healthy bit was all cloudy.

He was in on the Sunday and had the operation on the following Tuesday week. That week was tough because I don't think he was able to cope with being so scared. At least in the following few weeks when he was all cut up and drugged out of his head he didn't have the energy to fight but in those few days he'd just nag me about anything and everything every time I came in to visit. It was nasty. I thought for a while what was the point in coming in to visit. But he was my Da.

The weekend before the operation I just remembered I'd have to tell Gary about Da. There was no one to tell him except me. Hicksie or Ahmed from the shop would never think about getting in touch with Gary. They probably didn't even have his number. It would have to be me. I didn't want to have to drag him away from his scholarship but he had a right to know because it was his Da too.

Gary was in university in America because he was good at the discus. Talk about flukes. He won a couple of medals in the community games and next thing they were paying him to go to Boston for a few years to practise the discus and study some jokey American subject like psychology or something. Gary was the more athletic out of the two of us. He got the genes from his mother Siobhán who was Da's girlfriend before I was born. Da said Siobhán was good at swimming. We'd all seen her at other sports too – there was this tennis thing once – and she was all right. I had a different Ma. Even though

Da split up with Siobhán a couple of months after Gary was born, he met her loads of times since. I don't know much about my Ma. Gary doesn't either. She was going with Da for a while and then freaked out when she got pregnant and went off to London. She came back to Dublin to have me and then left me at this convent in Harold's Cross. Then Da took me back and brought me up with Gary.

The operation really did Da in. He looked awful overnight. The flesh caved in around his eyes and left grey circles and his eyebrows went up at angles on the inside and his skin sort of went see-through, all translucent. They didn't bother with the chemo because it was too late. The doctor didn't tell me and Gary it was too late but I knew because his hair didn't fall out. I saw that before in Lorraine. They didn't give her chemo either because it was too late. They did say he might live until Christmas but I knew it would only be weeks away. I bet if they didn't give him the operation at all he would have lived until Christmas and maybe longer. It just fucked him up. They shouldn't have done it at all. He lived the last few weeks with cancer. Instead he could have lived a few more months with just a bad flu.

I was there when the priest came in a couple of days before he died. I don't think they should have done that. It was morbid. Scary. I mean, Da was in a bad way but he was still probably aware of the priest, and he couldn't do anything because he was flat out on his back. If he'd been fully awake there would have been no way he'd have asked for a priest. It would have put the shits up him totally. I thought it was a bit sneaky. We were all Catholic but we weren't all that religious. We never really went to mass except at Christmas. I never heard Da pray really ever. The only thing he used to say was this thing with me and Gary when we were young before we went to bed. It was like, 'Star light, star bright, please keep me safe tonight.' And even that I think he got off a poem.

There was this bug going around the hospital those last few days which I didn't want to get; this MRSA thing.

I don't want to go into some shitty sob story about how I was close to my Da, because we weren't *that* close. I mean, we were close, but it was nothing special. It was just normal. We didn't need to throw any fucking baseballs around parks or anything. I didn't see him as some sort of hero. He was just my Da. I have this one thing which makes me a bit proud of him though. It's this photo taken in Amsterdam in the seventies before Gary was born with Da and my Uncle Phil and a couple of their mates. They're standing in this square with all these pigeons around them and they all have these sad hippy haircuts except for Da who has skint hair and this sort of army jacket dyed black. All the others are throwing bits of bread at these pigeons and they're smiling really goofily but Da is standing back from it all like 'I'm too cool for this' and he's got this fag in his mouth. But he really did look deadly and he was probably ahead of his time because he wasn't into all that hippy shit. He looked like a completely different person to when he was sick. Come to think of it he looked completely different to when I was growing up when he was narky and boring and on at me and he worked in this shitty carpet shop.

The funeral was really small. We have a tinchy family. There's just me and Gary and Uncle Phil who came over from Africa. Uncle Phil went to Nigeria ten years ago with this oil company he worked for in England and then married this

African woman and then got this job in the British Embassy of all places and never came back. It was funny because Da was beginning to get worried about him before he got married. That African woman was his first girlfriend. Da still didn't believe him until he sent over pictures to prove it. He told us that people in Africa think he's a missionary priest because he's Irish and some of his friends still call him Father Morris. He was only able to hang around for two days after the funeral because he had to go back to Nigeria for business. I missed him because he's interesting.

There were also a few people from the road there and Gary's Ma Siobhán and the lads from the shop, Da's boss Mr McHugh and Hicksie and Ahmed. I thought it was nice of Ahmed because he isn't even a Catholic. I don't think he's even a Christian. Gary was a bit pissed off at the turn-out for the whole ceremony. He told me so outside the church.

'Did you take care of the papers?' he said.

I told him I didn't know what he meant.

'The papers. Y'know – the *papers*. The *Evening Herald* death notices and all that. I thought I'd told you to ring them about Da. These things don't just get broadcast on their own.'

I thought *he*'d take care of stuff like that because he was older. He made me feel really guilty. I'd let Da down. I'd made it look like he had no mates. If there'd been an ad in the paper then more people might have come. Old school friends and those couple of girlfriends I remember Da having when I was younger. My Ma might have seen it too and she might have come.

TWO

I'm a pretty straight kind of guy. Wasn't it that Tony Blair who said that in his arsehole English accent? *I'm a pretty straight kind of guy.* Well that's me. I'd say I'm quite balanced. I don't think getting raised by only a Da and no Ma messed me up too much. Da had girlfriends living in the house before, but they just sort of stopped when I was about ten. The only one I really liked was called Bernie. I used to pretend to people in school she was my Ma. Any time the teacher would ask us to describe our Mas in class I'd say stuff about Bernie. I used to think she was my Ma. I think I *convinced* myself. I tried to call her 'Ma' but she'd get all embarrassed and Da would laugh and Gary would keep on calling her Bernie so it made me look thick. I used to wish that Bernie and Da would get married but it only lasted nine, ten months or something.

The only thing I would say is maybe I'm a little bit funny with girls. My secondary school was mixed. It was kind of tough because from the ages of nought to twelve I'd only talked to around five girls in my whole life. What made it worse was that after first year they stopped making us wear uniforms. Around the time I started they formed this student committee out of the sixth years and the transition years and they demanded that the pupils be allowed wear what they wanted. They thought they were the army or something, like student radicals. The worst thing was the teachers allowed all this to happen. They said it was about human rights. They were such dicks, the lot of them. I didn't mind wearing the uniform. You just wore the same clothes every day. It was one thing less to worry about in the mornings. Next thing school became this sort of fashion parade. The girls would only go for the blokes who wore what was in at the time. When I was in second year it was all that grunge gear: filthy check shirts and those beigey boot things. I didn't have a clue. I just had my Man United top and a couple of other things. And there was this cool way to act as well. It was like, 'I'm *so-o-o-o* depressed.' Blokes all drooping over with their hair long and covering their faces going, '*Wuuuuuuughh.*' I was like, 'Get your fucking act together.' And I wouldn't have minded, but most of these guys were the ones who were good at sport and were good at talking to girls. Designer depressed. They didn't need to get all depressed. But girls would still go for that sort of thing.

The only way I had a head start over the rest of the blokes was with the smoking. I could take it in like nobody else. I could feel the smoke sting the ring at the top of my lungs all right but I wouldn't cough. Everybody else when they started couldn't keep the smoke in without coughing. Most of them couldn't even inhale properly. They knew I could take it in because when I exhaled, the smoke came out in a thin blue stream like it had all the nicotine removed. When you breathe smoke out without taking it past your throat it comes out all puffy. I had one up on them there, and this was first year when I started. But the smoking wasn't enough after a while.

It was like they wrote down all the sound things about me on one side of a piece of paper and all the stuff they didn't agree with on the other side and there was more on the other side, like debit and credit, like in business studies. The other guys began to think I was smoking just to copy them. They forgot that I was one of the first. *They* were copying *me*! And anyway, smoking wasn't a show-off thing with me. I really needed to do it. I think I was dependent before I even began. It was just something to do with my hands.

I broke my arm around the Easter before the Junior Cert. This was some deal to me, one of those things I'd always dreaded. It wasn't the actual bone *breaking* in my arm which I was worried about most though. It was the cast. Getting my arm put in the cast and knowing that I'd have no mates to fill it up with signatures. This would show me up. This was the real test, the litmus. The girls wouldn't go for me and the blokes wouldn't respect me. Looking back I probably built it up into a worse thing than it actually was, but it really fucked with me at the time. I had one or two mates, but I couldn't have just one or two signatures because that would only draw attention to the fact that there was more *space* than writing on the plaster; and besides, my couple of friends were seen as dicks. I was thinking, 'Imagine just having Neil Doherty's signature on your arm.' Jesus. No. It was either *loads* of writing with *loads* of mad shit on it and girls' names and shit or no writing at all.

It was really freaky the way I broke my arm actually. It was such a nothing thing, just a trick I tried on Gary's old bike and the bottom of my arm went in an arc forward like a bow and went *snap!* You could actually *see* the muscle and the bone

coming out a bit, like raspberry ripple, the same colour. There
was this leaflet in the doctor's about osteoporosis. I always try
to drink a lot of milk now and take folic acid – one of the vita-
min Bs – in supplements.

I was really self-conscious about this cast and I'd try to hide
it by wearing long jumpers even though I remember it was
getting quite hot around that time that year. But it was pretty
thick. I mean, it must have been so obvious the way the knit
lines in my jumper would stretch and widen past the elbow. I
thought about just leaving it exposed and doing a couple of
signatures myself, but I'm right-handed and that was the arm
I broke.

'Be thankful for small mercies, Jer,' Da goes about it. 'They
can hardly make you write in class now.'

'Be thankful for small mercies,' Gary would say. 'At least
you won't go blind now.'

This one day in between geography and double maths I
thought I'd do something really mad with it. I don't know
where it came from; it just hit me. What I did was, I took
Dáire Macken's ruler from his desk when he wasn't looking
and stuck it down the space between my arm and the inside of
the cast so it was squashed up against the skin, soaking up all
the sweat and septic shit. The rest of the day he was going,
'Where the fuck's my ruler?' and he was really frantic because
this was a collector's item he said. It wasn't some Helix shat-
terproof shit. It had something like 'Eurodisney' printed on it
and it was one of the first rulers issued by Eurodisney when it
opened. It was really funny, because Dáire was always trying to
act the hard man and here he was, fifteen years of age or whatever, going ape-shit over a ruler.

At the end of the last class I decided to slide the ruler out from the cast. This was four o'clock, and it had been in there since half eleven. It was all yellow and there was steam coming off it if you held it up to a dark surface. When everybody got up to leave as the bell went, I swung a full hundred and eighty degrees and gave Dáire this vicious rasher with the ruler he'd been going mad about for the whole day. It made that *chick* sound that had everyone in the room go, '*Oooooh!*': 'Ooh!' with the pain and 'Ooh!' for 'Ooh, he's fucked, he's dead now.' Dáire grabs his arse and turns around and he's going, 'Morris, you fucking, *fucking* tit' and then he sees it was his ruler that did the damage and he sees the state it's in and he goes, 'Where the fuck has this been?' I should have given him some smart-arse answer like 'Up my hole' and been done with it, but I gave him this sad honest answer and held up my arm with the cast on it. I can't answer back in a cool way and I hate that. I hate that. Because I just wimped out I drew more attention to this clean white cast with no names on it.

Dáire Macken wasn't the kind of bloke to suffer someone getting one up on him. I knew I'd be dead. I was thinking and fretting about it later on at home.

'How's the mash there, Jer?' Da goes at dinner. 'You're not eating by the looks.'

'Ah, I am.'

'I've been in and out now three times in the last ten minutes, and that mound hasn't gone down. Is it the lumps again? The hard lumps. I haven't mashed out the lumps.'

'Nah, it's not the lumps, Da.'

'You need that female touch to mash out the lumps. I'm no good. I'm no good with that masher. It's only an old bockety yoke anyway. We'll get that, what is it, *For-Mash-Get-Smash* the next time.'

'It's not the lumps, Da.'

'You know what I told you about the Famine, Jer? If I had any brains I'd get offended by you not eating your mash. As an Irishman.'

'Da, no. I just don't feel too good. I've a funny stomach. I'm just thinking.'

There's this metal net they built at the bottom of the field in school for shot-putting and a bit of hammer throwing and discus. It was actually the first place Gary learned how to throw the discus. I was down there having a smoke the next day and this gang from my year starts coming down. I just stood there leaning against one of the posts holding up the net with this fag in my mouth like I didn't care what was going to happen, but I was really, totally, shitting it. I didn't want to lift my hand to my mouth to take out the fag and blow out the smoke because I knew my hand was shaking and I was afraid to show any signs. I just let it burn along towards the filter between my lips. The smoke was gathering in the space between the back of my mouth and my nose, tickling me and drying me up, and for the first time in a good while after however long of getting used to it and building up a resistance I felt like I was choking on smoke. There was Peter English in this gang and Dáire Macken was there of course and Greg McKenna and that little shit Ian Fuckface O'Halloran. The worst thing though was Peter English's girlfriend Melissa Freyne was with them. I just didn't want to be made a dick of in front of a girl.

The five of them stopped at the mouth of the net where the

concrete touches the grass and Peter English decides to become the spokesman because his bird is watching and he says something like, 'Did you break that arm from too much wanking Morris?' and I'm thinking to myself, 'Fuck you, English, you cunt', but I don't say anything and I take the end of the fag that's in my mouth like it's my instincts taking over and I flick it at his fucking ugly face.

Next thing I know, the five of them have me trapped in the inside of this net with no way out and the four lads are on top of me. Greg McKenna takes hold of the arm of my jacket and gets himself into the middle of the concrete circle moulded into the ground and starts to swing me around like I'm this hammer. He was a big fucker – way over six foot. If I'd been someone else and I was watching I actually would've been quite impressed because it took a lot of skill to do what he was doing. How he was doing it, there must have been quite a bit of resistance because my legs were scraping along the ground, but he still managed to get me around three, four, maybe five times. I thought he was going to let go towards the opening so I'd fly out on to the grass, but instead he makes me crash into the mesh. And then it was like, *bang*. My face is on the concrete and my arm with the cast on it is twisted up nearly over my head. I could feel the ball almost coming out of the pad. They were all cracking their shites. Through it all I could hear Melissa weaving over the top. I didn't think girls could find something like that funny. I got a few digs in the side and the legs and then they left because the quarter-to-eleven bell had gone about a minute before.

Then Peter English turns around again like he wants to make a final point. He walks back over and stands there over me sort of sniggering, with me sprawled out flat not saying anything.

'Any last requests, Morris? "A Million Green Bottles" or anything?'

'Huh?'

Then he takes out his cock and he pisses on me. *Literally* pisses on me. I couldn't believe it. Right in front of Melissa and everything.

I'm not sure what really annoyed me more in the long run though – getting pissed on or finding 'JEROME MORRIS IS A QUEER' written in big thick marker on my cast. That was their original plan I'd say. The pissing and getting thrown around were spur-of-the-moment things but writing 'JEROME MORRIS IS A QUEER' was their original plan. You don't just bring a big thick marker around for no reason. I could have bet it was Dáire Macken who did it too. Revenge for the ruler. I fucking hated that. I fucking hated them thinking I was a queer just because I was nervous with girls or that I'd never had a girlfriend or anything. It was like, if something isn't one thing then it's completely the opposite. I fucking hated that. I mean, I could've tippexed over the writing, but it wouldn't have mattered because they'd all have gone around telling everyone they'd written it still. This would be my reputation down the bog. It started to get to me. I even began telling people that I *did* have a girlfriend before and her name was Lorraine. I suppose in effect she was sort of a girlfriend although we never actually said it. I started to feel a bit guilty because I was thinking maybe it was disrespect for the dead.

My life was looking like it was going to be hell for a few weeks, but then coming up closer to the Junior Cert I got

lucky. I found out this girl in fifth year fancied me. She was in
fifth year but she wasn't that much older than me because
she'd skipped transition year. Her friend came up to me in the
queue for the long jump on sports day in April. She was able
to know where I'd be by looking at the list pinned up on the
notice board. She told me about her friend and what she
thought about me and that her name was Cynthia. She said
she was sound. I didn't like that name though. It reminded me
of old women with powder in their wrinkles and too much eye
make-up going in clumps. *O-o-oh Cynthia, will you ever put on
the potatoes there?* She pointed to Cynthia across the field,
lining up for the ladies' 400 metre heats. I'd noticed this particular girl before. She took half the same route as me home on
her lunch break and usually would have done after school too,
but recently she'd been staying back for extra study time, her
friend said. But there was something else familiar about her, I
thought.

I'd caught her making eye contact with me before, I remembered. It was between classes one day, when both of us were
hanging up our jackets on the same rack. People tell me my
best features are my eyes, that you can't avoid them, that
they're all sort of *blue*. She was locked in my line of vision, like
a tractor beam. I thought she was just staring at me because of
my gawky blue eyes. But now this was a whole different story.
She must have been on to me for ages.

She was good looking all right. Not a total ride or anything. But she was good looking, and once I knew she fancied
me I started to fancy her.

It seemed like most of the effort was gone now. It was great.
There'd be no messing around trying to push myself on to her.

She was dead into me and I knew her friend wasn't bullshitting. This sort of thing happened to me before, just the one time, when I was in first year, but I wasn't ready for it. I got notes passed to me but I felt a bit freaked out. I felt like *I* should have been making all the moves if anything like this ever happened, the way I'd planned it, being a bloke; but here was this bird hunting me out from a distance, some bird I didn't even know, hunting and plotting and passing me notes. I don't know. I felt ready this time though. This was it. The big one. All I had to do was show I was interested, stick my chest out or whatever and then it'd be hook, line and sinker, and all that.

Her friend told me she liked quiet guys. She got the impression I was all arty and sensitive just because I seemed shy. I played that game for a while so. I don't know how she didn't cop on immediately. I mean, I was in Mr Cleland's *pass* English class for the *Junior* Cert and she was in Mrs Alderdice's *honours* class for the *Leaving*. But I found out within the first two weeks she was a bit of a spoofer and that the only things she knew about James Joyce or whatever else she kept going on about were the names of the books they wrote. She hadn't actually read any of them. She only even got a 'C' in the Junior Cert for English.

I suppose it was all rocky foundations when I think about it, all negative. But you feel like more than just a couple when it's based on something like that. You feel like it's two people against the world. Backs to the wall sort of stuff with machine-guns going *yeah, yeah!* Cynthia hated all the things about school I hated. She thought the no-uniform rule was crap. She hated staying in for lunch. She hated French too, although she only hated it because she was no good at it even though she wished she was, but I hated it because I was no good at it *and* because of Mr Torrance *and* because it was a faggotty language. When I pressed her she had to admit it was a faggotty language too. *Ooooh! Ou est le poo poo pee pee la de da?* She wasn't doing any business subjects for the Leaving because Mr Casey had been a total prick for business studies for the Junior Cert. When I'd filled out the form for what subjects I'd be picking for the Leaving Cert, I'd avoided all the business subjects because of Mr Casey, although I'd have liked to do accounting because it would have been useful. She also told me to try to avoid Mr Manus for Irish because he used this Donegal Irish which nobody could understand. I told her there'd be no danger of that because I'd be doing pass Irish.

Both of us had fairly similar tastes in other shit too. She liked the Stone Roses even though she thought their last album was shite except for the singles and 'Tightrope'. She hated rave music although I remember we both agreed that 'No Limits' by 2Unlimited was good. We both *despised* grunge music. She tried to get me into the Smiths and shit but I must have been missing something. I preferred Blur. She didn't like football either and she didn't smoke. I told her the build-up to the '94 World Cup made me happy and the aftermath made me depressed. She thought the opposite she said. I told her I'd been on a downer since the Irish team got shit. She thought it was great that the Charlton bubble had burst.

Da was great about it. I thought he'd hit the roof like everyone else's Da might if their son started going out with someone just before the Junior Cert. But I should have known. Da was sound like that. He said that the Junior Cert

was bollocks. It wasn't important and no employer gave a shite
about it. It was just about government statistics. How brainy
Irish fifteen-year-olds were compared to other European countries and all that. It had a different name in his day, but it was
bollocks then and it's bollocks now he said. He asked me what
I liked about Cynthia. I told him it was her general attitude to
things. She was a hater. Hate, hate, hate. Hate this, hate that.
A cynic. I don't know, it was different. It wasn't all sugar and
spice.

'Ah, good man,' he said, laughing, 'you've got the same
tastes as your old lad.'

And then I said I didn't mean to be all poncey – and I
know this sounds all poncey – but I think she loved me.

'You what?'

And I *don't* mean to be a ponce but she did. And at the start
I think she really did, I swear. There might have been a bit of
something in return, I'm not sure. It started off with a bit of
panic and worry because I didn't really know about birds and
women and shit and how to act, but then it turned into a
warm feeling in my blood system, like probably the hormones
taking over. It was like this new adventure for both of us, and
both of us were going into it for the first time.

But then we got bored. I don't know, other people might be
able to motivate themselves, but I just find it hard to make
myself excited about things for nothing. I think maybe I'm a
bit autistic, even though I'm not even good at maths or
drawing.

THREE

I think things sort of changed for me and Cynthia after my seventeenth birthday. We'd gone out drinking for the night. I know I hadn't reached the legal age and all that yet but I'd been going out to pubs for a year anyway, so it was no big deal. It was 30 September and only a few weeks after Da had died. I didn't feel much different.

Cynthia had put me in a bad mood from the start that night. She'd given me this dark green polo-neck thing and a video, *The Best of RPM Motorsport*, and five pounds worth of prize bonds as a present, and because I hadn't said thanks immediately she was going, 'So you don't like your present then' and I went, 'No, I do', and because I didn't put more emphasis on the word 'do', she thought I was just being polite and wasn't a good-enough actor to hide the fact that I didn't think much of her present. Even though I did; the *thought* of it. For the whole of the walk from the bus stop to Sinnott's I was trying to stress to her how grateful I was, and because she was just charging ahead looking down at the path, I thought I wasn't getting through to her, so I started to sound all aggressive, except all I was doing was raising my voice a bit to get a few points across. And then she turns around to me at the door of the pub and she goes, 'Don't you fucking shout at me in public.' And there was she, shouting at *me* in public, right in front of the bouncer and all the people looking much older going in and out. It's a wonder we even got in.

The change in the atmosphere calmed her down a bit. It was too noisy to continue arguing. It was too noisy but I could see she was still in a huff. I didn't know what was worse. I'd have preferred to take it head on than to put up with a sulk for the night. We made our orders and found some seats just as people got up to leave, and we prepared to dig in for the night.

I could never understand how Cynthia could get herself into such bad moods. She'd snap into them and stay stuck in this rut for hours. Most people might loosen up a bit with a few drinks on them, but with Cynthia, she'd get more intense. I tried to lighten up the situation by doing the music for the Guinness ad every time I'd lift my pint to my mouth, all that twangy harp thing. I was doing it in an annoying way on purpose, to get a reaction out of her. She told me to shut up and stop being so immature and that anyone would swear I hadn't just turned eighteen. I told her I hadn't, I'd just turned seventeen. If that was *me* who'd forgotten *her* age, the shit would have *completely* hit the fan. And there was this other word she kept on using that night: 'trivial'. She told me to stop being so *trivial* about everything.

We were both well on the way to getting pissed. It was like we were going for self-destruct. The two of us knew we weren't going to enjoy ourselves. There wasn't a gang of us there or anything. We couldn't bounce off anyone else. Just two people in a bad mood in this tense atmosphere. We were both drinking to get out of our skulls. I wasn't saying anything and she wasn't saying anything. I looked around. There were all these dicks in rugby shirts, all obviously in the same team, with letters stitched on their backs in these cloth diamonds. I counted a 'J', an 'F', a 'H' and a 'B'. I tried to get Cynthia to help me out to get up to 'Z', or the fifteenth letter of the alphabet, or however many people there are on a rugby team, but she wasn't interested. I let out this fart by accident. I held my breath. I didn't think Cynthia heard me.

There was some eighties crap playing on the stereo.

I looked down at my present on the seat. I didn't even know what prize bonds were for. She mentioned something about her parents, the Farrellys, having them and about how it was a family tradition or some shit. And where Cynthia got that video from – or *why* even – I just couldn't work out. I wasn't even *into* cars.

She went back up to the bar to get another pint. She didn't ask me did I want another one. There were three empty glasses on her side of the table and four on mine and I was bored out of my mind.

Then she started doing the giggles. Giggles is too nice a word for it. It was her nasty little laugh. It always happened when she was drunk. She'd start giggling to herself and then come out with the most hurtful thing she could think of about me. It was usually something that was pretty honest, something that had been nagging her for ages. This time she confused me though. She was supping back on her pint like normal and then she held it in suspension in front of her face, staring into it, with a bit of head dripping off the tip of her nose, like she was thinking about something. She was swishing liquid backwards and forwards into her mouth, not really drinking, just gurgling, making bubbles in her drink with her laughing. She was making a show of herself. I mean, I'm not some dry-arse PC merchant, but really. For a girl.

'What's wrong?' I said.

'What's wrong?! What's fucking wrong?! I'll tell you what's wrong,' she said, slamming the glass back down on the table like she's in some fucking film. And then she pinched the bridge of her nose and squinted her eyes up and I wasn't sure for a second whether she was laughing or crying until she opened her mouth and I realized she was laughing.

'September the thirtieth . . .' She stopped and there was more of this hysterical laughing. She had to catch herself and draw her breath to compose herself and continue. She was wearing too much make-up.

'I was just thinking. September the thirtieth . . . mmm . . . minus nine months . . .'

She was now crumpled over on the seat laughing into the curve of her wrist. I felt like I should have been getting something but I just wasn't. That New Order song that goes 'How does it feel . . .' came on and I thought 'Fuck it' and went up for a dance on my own.

I'm quite a good dancer actually. I've got a good ear for a beat. I can do this thing with my arms like a snake. It starts off on my left hand and I make a wave go all the way up my arm, across my shoulders and down the other arm. I roll my head as the wave goes by my neck. With proper lighting it would have looked deadly, under a strobe. I was giving it loads that night, doing all my moves. This girl came up and started dancing in front of me, sort of wiggling vertically with her arms up in the air, while I was doing my sideways thing. I was fucking loving it. I looked over at Cynthia to catch the look on her face but she was gone from her seat. I thought I'd impress this girl more by moving my hips around and grabbing my crotch and shifting my hand up and down. I sort of cupped my hand to make it look like I was holding this huge package. She came up closer to me and whispered something in my ear but I couldn't hear what she was saying above all the noise.

The bass was beginning to hurt my liver. I could feel my insides actually vibrating around, going *boom boom* with the bass. I thought I'd show off to this girl even more, even though now she seemed to be turned towards someone else. I went up to her at the end of the next song and said I was going to go up to get her and me two drinks and tell the guy behind the bar to turn the bass down. I thought she'd be kind of impressed by that. Not many people know technical terms like bass or whatever. I knew about it because Hicksie was really into music and he got this stereo installed into the shop with these huge bass speakers, these sub-woofters or something. I thought I'd go up to the guy and show this girl I meant business and that I knew what I was talking about.

I ordered another Guinness for myself and I just sort of assumed to order a Pernod and lime for this girl. I'd forgotten to even ask her what she wanted but my instincts told me that a Pernod and lime was the thing to get. While I was waiting for my pint to settle I shouted at the guy to turn the bass down. 'The *fucking* bass down.' I wanted to make it sound more aggressive.

'Hey, turn that fucking bass down, will you?!'

I leaned full stretch over the bar to get my hands on the graphic equalizer. But the barman just started to get all panicky

then, like I was going to rip off his till. The dick went and
grabbed me by the wrist and tried to push me back over the
bar, but most of my body was over the other side, so he just
pulled me behind instead. Then he starts waving over towards
the bouncer to take care of me. I thought for a minute I'd had
it. But the bouncer was a joke. He gave me this spiel about
some fucking crap. About how we all like to have a good time
and to take things easy and to go back and enjoy myself.

I went back up to the bar to get the drinks. The Pernod and
lime was still there and I just took the nearest freshly pulled
pint of Guinness that was lying on the bar. I couldn't see that
girl anywhere. I thought I'd play the old drunken poet thing.
Go over and mope in a corner with a drink in each hand like
I'm Pat's Hat or something, like I'm above it all.

I spotted Cynthia again. She was doing almost exactly the
same sexy dancing thing that that girl was doing with me with
this other bloke, this rugger-bugger dick. He looked like a
seven foot twelve-year-old pumped up with muscles, with cau-
liflower ears, and those lips. I knocked back the Pernod whole
and started walking over towards them with half my pint left,
swirling around in the glass, looking like I had a few stern
words to say.

When I got closer I couldn't believe it. The bloke was wearing the polo neck that Cynthia gave me. Cynthia looked like
she was having a great laugh because the polo neck was about
ten sizes too small for the guy and he was dancing like a dick.
It was almost like they were taking the piss out of my body.
Cynthia made him lean down towards her so she could whis-
per something in his ear. She was still in hysterics. The bloke
took off the polo neck, looking down at me like I'm this piece

of shit. He was wearing a rugby shirt underneath. He turned around to dance with Cynthia again. There was this big 'C' stitched on his back. 'C' for fucking 'cunt', I thought.

I said to myself, 'Fuck the polo neck.' I was thinking, 'Fuck the video and the prize bonds too.' Wherever they were. I really wanted to leave.

On my way out I saw the video on the ground. It was out of its box and all smashed up. I stamped down on it with my heel and smashed it up more. I kept on stamping and smashing, stamping and smashing. Then I picked up the reel of film and ripped off a length with my teeth and wrapped it round my arm and made for the door. 'I Am The Resurrection' was finishing up on the stereo. I turned around to shout 'Fuck the lot of you', except with 'yiz' instead of 'you' to make it sound better. I thought the song was over but then that twiddly guitar bit at the end started up and my shouting was drowned out. The bouncer just grabbed me and threw me out, literally, like a sack of potatoes or something.

'*September the thirtieth minus nine months*,' I was thinking to myself on the Nitelink. I kind of knew what she was getting at but I didn't let it get to me. I was pissed and I was enjoying the buzz in my head. I just knew that those words would destroy me in the morning. It was weird. I knew that they'd get to me in the morning even though I was aware of what they meant now but I was pissed so it didn't matter.

Everyone was smoking on the top deck. Nobody cares about the no-smoking rule on buses when it's the Nitelink. The drivers are too scared to take on a bus load of pissed-up gurriers over some little rule. I lit up myself. It was hilarious.

The driver decided to sort it out this time. '*Once and for all,*' he was probably thinking to himself, '*I'm gonna show them who's boss around here.*' The bus stopped to a halt and the weediest little shit ever comes walking up the stairs really slowly going *thud, thud* with his feet on the steps to make it sound like he was bigger than he was. It was so funny. He had a neck like a gimp.

'All right now, listen. You're gonna have to put out the smokes or else I'm gonna get the police. The garda station is only two minutes away. All right?'

It was like, 'Oh we're *shitting* ourselves.' And his voice was actually *shaking* towards the end of the sentence. He totally bottled it. He was just asking for someone to give him some shit.

I felt this sort of blood rush. I jumped out of my seat and stood there in front of him with my legs wide apart and both my hands pointed at him like pistols, moving backwards and forwards doing that ra-ta-ta-tat thing.

'F-U-C-K Dub-lin Bus!'

And he puts his hands up to his face like he's trying to protect himself. Like I'm *actually* shooting him!

'Eff, Yoo, See, Kay, Dub-lin Bus!'

It was crazy. He actually runs back down the stairs and starts the engine back up and continues on with the route. As if nothing happened! I'd completely rattled him.

I was the hero of the hour. Everybody was cheering and clapping like it's Hollywood or something. This crowd of blokes started singing 'Molly Malone', but when they got to the bit that goes '. . . as she wheeled her wheelbarrow through the streets broad and narrow crying . . .', they shouted

'Blackrock! Blackrock!' instead of 'cockles and muscles'. I started to conduct them, moving my hands up and down like I had one of those sticks. I did the moonwalk up and down the aisle and that thing with my crotch again. I was shouting 'Whooaa!' and 'Oooh baby!' and shit and everyone was thinking I'm deadly.

When it came to my stop, I took the piss out of the driver again as I passed him. I was singing that song we used to sing in the playground in primary.

'C-I-E are rob-ber-y, Doo Dah, Doo Dah.'

Taunting and jeering him and giving him V-signs. It was mad.

It was a cold night. I was aware but I didn't really notice it. I could see my breath going all steamy in the air. The headlights of the cars were blurred with the fog. It's hard enough to judge the distance of cars just going by their headlights on a normal night, but the mist makes it worse. I wasn't even looking left or right when I stood off the grass in the middle of the dual-carriageway on to the tarmac, just dead ahead. Then something stopped me. Something. I took a step back again. My head and eyes were still fixed rigid in the same position. This car whizzed by me with its horn blaring. It brushed me gently. I could feel the surge of air. *Whooosh*. Close one. That was the star light star bright working I thought.

I was thinking about what Cynthia said again. I looked down at my right foot. The sole of my shoe was coming off, flapping like a flip-flop. I started making quacking noises because it looked like a duck. My sock was getting wet. There was this bush going all the way up the road with dew on the leaves. I moved my arm through it as I walked. Now my sleeve was getting wet. I didn't feel the wetness.

I tried to think of all the counties in Ireland that began with 'C'. I got three. Then I tried the same with 'S'. I could only think of one. I was surprised. Then I moved on to countries. Sweden. Spain. Scotland. Sudan. Switzerland. Sahara. Spain. Cyprus. Cleland is Scottish. He said that all the main men of the British Empire were either Scottish or Irish. He said we all have blood on our hands.

I got home. I put the key in the door. I went to bed.

'*September the thirtieth minus nine months.*'

I woke up with the munchies. I'm always like that with a hangover. I just have to eat. It was half one p.m. when I looked at the clock. There was no way I was going to school. I was stupid to even think I was going to be able to go out, get hammered and still be in a state to go to school the next day.

There were two pains also. The first was in my mouth and there was a taste of copper or something. It wasn't really a pain. It was a soreness, an irritation. My mouth was full with something. I felt like I was going to gag. I was nearly choking on something. I put my fingers in my mouth and took out my key to the house. I couldn't believe it. I'd actually done it. I remembered reading somewhere that if you sleep with a key under your tongue it cures hangovers. I couldn't believe I actually did that. It just shows you. The stupid things you do when you're pissed. It frightened me.

The other pain was in my ribs. I lifted up my shirt and there was this huge bruise like the map of Africa. I couldn't remember how I'd got it.

I wanted to stuff my face. I had half of this big slab of Whole Nut left over from when Uncle Phil was here, a couple of these mini buns and these two rolls for breakfast. I was just standing there at the fridge loading all this crap into my mouth. I forgot about the nuts in the Whole Nut. It wasn't going down too well. I could feel my stomach beginning to turn.

I needed to neutralize the acids or whatever. There's this medicine cupboard above our counter which we never restock. It has all rose-water and shit in it from God knows. I started to look for Alka Seltzers. I'd never used them before but I needed something like that now. Da used to take them for his heartburn. They probably worked better than keys I figured. I found this little blue packet that looked like a pack of johnnies. I ripped it open and popped two in my mouth. I started to chew but it made me feel worse. It was all frothy. I heard a noise behind me. It was Gary. He must have heard me in the kitchen.

'What the fuck is all that shit coming out of your mouth?'

I mumbled something that I think sounded like 'Alka Seltzer'.

'Aw, you fucking dick stain. You're meant to put those things in water. Here, give us a look.'

He went over to the cupboard.

'Ah Jesus. Those were the last ones. Fuck. Anyway, happy birthday Jer.'

He handed me this long, flat present which had been lying up in the gap between the fridge and the press.

'I'm sorry, I completely fucking forgot about it yesterday. I only remembered to buy something just before the shops closed yesterday, and by then you were gone. Sorry.'

It was this big framed picture of Roy Keane. This cardboard print with a gold plastic frame. It was nice of Gary. I mean, it was the kind of present you'd give a ten-year-old, but it was really nice of him all the same. He needn't have bothered. I wasn't expecting anything off him. He said he had stuff to do in town and he'd be back later. It was nice of him.

My stomach was in knots again. There were these clammy sweats. It was just this wave of sickness starting in my stomach and spreading out. It was like stones dropping into a pond, with the stones getting bigger and the waves getting stronger and the spray getting higher. I needed to get to the toilet fast.

I always hate the feeling of getting sick. You think you're going to die. It's such a violent thing. But after you've puked then there's this relief. There's this great feeling of peace.

It was pretty fierce this time though. It hit the toilet so fast that the water from the bowl churned and splashed up. It was that stingy puke too that clogs up your nose and gives you tears. Really stingy stomach-acid puke mixed with Guinnessy blackness. My teeth were all grainy. It made me feel chilly and alone. I hadn't puked in so long. The last time, Da held his hand on my brow to take the weight off the force of the puking. It was like a lever. That sort of thing was comforting. If I had a temperature then Da's hand would feel nice and cool, but if I was cold and shivery then his hand would seem warm. He used to do that when we were kids with me and Gary, and Bernie used to do it too. It wasn't a kid's thing to want something like that when you were more grown up. It had a practical purpose. I needed something like that now.

I needed to dab my face with cold water. I was lucky I checked the sink before I put my hands in it. It was all blocked

up with puke and there was a pool of vomit in it. It looked like
there were half-tomatoes and little chrysanthemums in there.
It looked like Gary had been puking too.

Things were beginning to settle down. The window in our
kitchen was weird. It took up almost the whole side of the
room and it seemed to catch the rain. It kind of hypnotized
and relaxed you. Whatever way the rain fell on it, it was sort of
held there and swirled around. It made funny shapes with the
light in the kitchen.

Then I remembered again.

'*September the thirtieth minus nine months.*'

September the thirtieth minus nine months is New Year's
Eve. I counted again. September, August . . .

It definitely was. No matter what way you looked at it.
That's when Da and my Ma did it. That's when I was con-
ceived or whatever. New Year's Eve. There's no love in that. It
must have been just a drunken thing. Slap, bang, wallop. At a
party or something. A piss-up. It was all just an accident. I
wasn't meant to be. I just wasn't meant to happen. Da probably got the fright of his life when my Ma told him.

I cried and I screamed and I just wanted to fucking die.

*I never wanted to smoke again. I never wanted to touch a
drink again. I never wanted to see Cynthia again. I didn't need
that kind of love right then.* I just wanted comfort. I wanted to
be innocent. I didn't want to have to worry about anything. I
wanted to be protected. I wanted to be like a little kid again.
I wanted a Ma and a Da and a happy house.

I spent the rest of the day watching my football videos. I have
the '94 and '96 Cup Finals on tape. I also have this special video

about the Double in '94. I watched *The Team That Jack Built*. Then I put on this video we have about Chris Waddle. He's my favourite player ever, although he never played for United and I can't really remember him at his peak. I even put on this video of the 1990 FAI Cup Final between Bray Wanderers and St Francis. The standard is so bad. I don't know where we got it. I think Da picked it up from some bargain bin somewhere. He's originally from Bray. I started to watch this Channel 4 Italian football video also, but I couldn't finish it because it just reminded me of Sundays.

2

FOUR

I went about a month and then lit another cigarette. The thing was, I wasn't making this conscious effort to stay off the fags or anything. It wasn't like the pledge or Lent or a swear box. I just didn't want to smoke for those couple of weeks and I felt good about it. I got my comfort from somewhere else.

I got my comfort from just going to school every morning and looking forward to getting home and then coming in the door and putting on the Super Ser and the heat and the smell. It was the most comforting feeling in the world that – drying off your wet clothes in front of the Super Ser while they were still on you and catching the whiff of the gas. It wasn't a druggy thing, a buzz thing, or getting high on the gas or anything. Just the sort of feelings that that would trigger off. Those homely sort of feelings. The feeling that your homework was still at least half an hour away because you had no choice but to dry out and the feeling that there was good kids' TV on at that time just before the news and that you wouldn't get a cold but you might get chilblains because your clothes were going all starchy on your limbs from the wet heat.

It's funny. The Super Ser used to scare the hell out of me too. That purring noise and the way the metal sheets used to rattle. I always worried when I was a kid that it would blow up or we'd all choke on the gas. I remember screaming at Da every time he lit a fag in the room. Or there was that other thing. Da would go up behind the Super Ser and grip it by the sides and go, '*Ticktock, ticktock.*'

'Blue wire or red wire Jer? Will I cut the blue or the red?'

And I'd be going, 'Red! Red! No, no . . . blue!'

'Come on Jer, one or the other. Red or blue? Quick now! *Ticktock, ticktock . . .*'

'Blue Da, blue! Definitely blue.'

And then he'd go '*Shick*' and there'd be silence and shock, like this knack of making himself *look* like he was actually sweating, *actually* in a bit of a panic.

'Wrong wire! Wrong wire! Duck Jer, head down! She's gonna blow!'

And then I'd dive in behind the bean bag and Da would make an explosion noise and that Japanese dying sound in comics, that '*Aieeeeee!*' sound. And I'd be genuinely scared. Genuinely thinking this thing was going to blow.

But it is funny. It's funny the way some things you don't enjoy as they happen but when you remember them they just make you happy. Most stuff, so long as it's only a bit shit and not *totally* shit, is okay once you survive it. Once it's in your past and it was harmless enough you can look back at it and say, 'Yeah, that was a happy time.' It's all sort of nostalgia. You just remember it as happy. The trick is letting things settle down with time or whatever.

I did my homework every evening for those couple of weeks lying down on the floor in the living room on the rug. I used to do my colouring books like this when I was little and just sink into the white fur. Sometimes I'd press my ear down against it and think I could hear this monster breathing all heavy or its heart going *vwum, vwum*. Me and Gary used to have mess scraps on the rug. We used to scrap each other *and* the rug! We used to pretend it was a polar bear or a gremlin. Now I was about ten times bigger than the rug but it didn't matter. It was just the idea. The sameness. The pattern of it all and the comfort and all that.

The last couple of months was different every day. All turmoil. Chaos and shit. This was always the same every day but it was brilliant. No. No, it was *nice*. Just *nice*. I thought about Da a bit but it didn't cut me up. That was nice too. It wasn't even sadness. It was just . . . *feelings*. I wouldn't say I'd be scared if I ever saw a ghost. It was like there were rays coming up off the carpet.

But fuck it.

Fuck it, fuck it. I had to say, 'Fuck it.' I was acting like a total ponce. It was time to grit my teeth and just get on with things and act my age. I was like, 'Get a hold of yourself, man.' Fuck's sake. What was I thinking? A big hug from somewhere? *A-ah. Pooor Jer.* I needed to kick myself up the hole. *Seventeen years of age.* Fuck's *sake*.

We needed bread, so I went over to The Mews to get sliced pan. It was pissing down as I was walking back through Summerfield. The footpaths are a state in our area. There was all this muck and worms bubbling up from the cracks and spreading over the concrete. The council are a disgrace. They're always off on their strikes and no work ever gets done. Everyone should get together and sue shit out of them. There's this one spot on the path where the road out of Twelve Bens meets the road leading up to our estate and I *always* slip on this one spot without fail *all the time* coming home from the shops. This day it's no exception. It's like, I could see it coming because it's on a slant, but no, I *still* stand on it and then I slip and I fall backwards and I nearly smash my brains and get killed and I get soaked. I hate shit like that. It's not the pain, it's the embarrassment.

Of all the times for something like that to happen then, someone I know goes by. I was picking myself up, shaking the wet off the sleeve of my jacket and rubbing the bone at the top of my arse which I thought I'd shattered when all of a sudden there's this beam through the drizzle. I can't make anything out for a second because the headlights are shooting right into the backs of my eyeballs like a fox, but next thing a car door swings open and I hear this 'Hey, Jeece, Jerome Morris. Come on in and I'll give you a lift the rest of the way.' It was one of Gary's old mates, Neville Carbury. No, I thought. What'll I say to him? I hadn't talked to him in years. He was just trying to be a Flash Harry with his car, like 'I'm the head honcho around here.'

'Nah, it's all right Neville. I could do with the walk. Y'know, the exercise and shit.'

'Exercise? Well, Jeece. You're thin enough. It's fucking bucketing too. But what the fuck. Your choice, man.'

The wet was hard to shake off my sleeve. It seemed the rain was getting heavier the last minute, driving and driving, right into my bones. Shit anyway, I thought. *Yeah*, shit. A lift's a lift.

'Eh. Actually, yeah Neville. If you're going that way.'

There was that awkward silence in the car. I looked over at Neville for a second thinking maybe he was jittery and sending out these vibes, but he was cool and calm. He was just concentrating on the road.

'That's funny music there Neville. It's all old.'

'Yeah. I have a mate who deejays a lot down some place out near Blessington. Country 'n' western nights. Inherited all the gear from his old man. PA, big stack of forty-fives, the lot. I just gave him a whole load of blank tapes and asked him to fill her up. Makes a change from the usual shit I have on.'

Both of us laughed. Neville lit up a fag. The second he took his first draw it was like *ooh, come to Daddy* – the sweet smell of nicotine.

'Bread, yeah?' he asked.

'Yeah. Bought it in the shop.'

'Here, d'you want one of these?'

I looked at the cigarette he was offering and slinted my eyes.

'Nah. Trying to stay off.'

'Fair enough.'

We were coming into my estate.

'Sorry about your old man, by the way. Only heard about it the other week. Rough.'

'Thanks.'

'Here we are. This is the one, isn't it?'

'This is the one.'

'Say hello to your sister for me, will you?'

'Don't have a sister.'

Neville looked confused for a second.

'Jeece. I'm getting you mixed up with someone else.'

'No, it's Gary you know.'

'Oh yeah, Jeece. Gary. Yeah. Say hello.'

'Will do.' I stopped as I got out of the car. 'Here. Is it too late to ask for a fag?'

'Ye cheeky fucking pup! Go 'way with ye!'

'Ah sorry. I shouldn't really anyhow.'

'Will you come back here you fucking eejit! Take one. Take *two*!'

Somebody I hadn't talked to for two years or something, and I ask him for a fag. That was it; I was gone. I knew I was a smoker again. I stood in the porch and sucked the little fucker half-way down through its filter. I could actually feel the heat coming off it. It was like, 'Welcome back.' It was like those ads where all those kids glow up all red after eating Ready Brek. I walked the whole way back to The Mews in the rain and the muck to buy a packet of twenty Silk Cuts and that was it. Back on the fags.

It only hit me a couple of weeks after Da's funeral about Gary. He was still hanging around. I'd forgotten completely about his scholarship. I thought he might have forgotten as well, but fuck, as if you'd forget something like that. Maybe the shock of Da had shaken his mind up, but it wasn't like he was acting all strange or anything. He had it all sorted out though. The plan was he was going to take the year off and stay home for a while he said. Take stock. I hoped he wasn't doing it for my sake.

It was weird the way things worked out between me and Cynthia. She got offered this course pretty late off the CAO. Somebody dropped out and she got this place on some computer course down in Carlow. She'd stalled on her second choice. She got given this trout-farming thing in some college down the country but then she stalled and didn't take it up. It was so thick of her. I couldn't understand. Why did she put it down in the first place if there was a chance she was going to get it?

I'd love something like that, to have a trout farm down the country somewhere. It sounds really weird, like a room in Willy Wonka's factory where they make all trouts and shit, or that thing on April Fool's Day years ago when they conned all these people into thinking there were spaghetti farmers in Switzerland. But there's a big demand for them. There's this trout farm down in Wicklow where me and Da and Gary used to go. You'd pay a couple of quid and they'd give you this shitty rod like a green garden cane with no reel. There was this bait that the trout would go mad for. Actually, it tasted all right for humans too. But the trout would go completely mad for it. It was like that piranha film. Hoards of them swarming around your hook, churning the water, like their life depended on it, like they couldn't get enough. You'd always go home with this Dunnes bag full of fish, every time. It was like toy-fishing, like gnomes. It was mad. The knackers had it sussed though. They were real knackers, culchie knackers, with all orange hair and that accent. They used to nick the trout with yellow string off this bridge that went over the stock pools. The owners would come running out of these sort of road workers' huts going, 'Ye little shits, ye little fucking shits', but the knackers would get away every time. I always thought I'd like to own a place like that. It wouldn't cost much to keep, and not only would you get money from people bringing their kids down to go fishing, but you'd also get paid to stock up rivers and sell fish to supermarkets. It wouldn't take a genius to run one, like someone like me could do it, but you'd maybe need to go to college to do fish breed-ing and how to make water pure, and science. And you wouldn't need much staff. It'd just be you and the fish and you'd be down in the country.

So off she went to this place down in Carlow to do her computer course. She didn't need to think twice about it. I met her every weekend for the next four weeks.

Actually, I forgot. The weekend before the weekend we split up she stayed down in Carlow.

Cynthia's Da was really decent. A decent old skin, as my own Da used to say. '*Salt of the earth!*' I was like this second son to him and Mrs Farrelly, but maybe I'm looking at the whole sit-uation all wonky. Cynthia's brother Martin was away in college up in the North, like Gary, only he had a real excuse. He *had* brains; there was none of this messing about. He'd found him-self some bird up there and he was off skiing in Scotland and only came down every once in a while leaving Cynthia to be the one to come home every weekend for their Ma and Da. Martin was sound enough too, but he always made me feel a bit funny. Maybe it was because he was nearly around the same age as me, and here I was, messing around with his sister; I don't know. It was just sort of tense. While he was away, Mr Farrelly was all pals with me and giving me that 'How's it goin'?!' punch on the shoulder and all, 'Did you see United last week?' Mostly when people had been doing that kind of thing recently I'd be thinking they were just trying to treat me as normal as possible after Da, but really, behind it all, there were the usual feelings. But with Mr Farrelly, it was like I was slotting into the space where Martin should have been. I even went to see Shels with him one Friday night, and that was like this ritual between him and Martin, going to Tolka Park to see Shels play on a Friday or Saturday or whatever.

But this other Friday, the Friday of the weekend that things ended between me and Cynthia, me and Mr Farrelly were going to the bus station in town. I'd just been over to drop some model paints back to Mr Farrelly when Cynthia rang from some place that the bus's tyre had blown out down the country somewhere saying she'd be home soon and Mr Farrelly said he'd pick her up from town and both of us hopped in the car and went down to that Busáras.

I couldn't believe it when I saw her get off the bus. Me and Mr Farrelly were waiting around in these pools of oil where all the buses pull in and Cynthia comes climbing down the steps of the bus with this woolly top on and this bag swinging around like the Arabs would drink water out of in the desert, only bigger, for books and copies. Mr Farrelly went into shock. Then the two of us just started cracking our shites. *Cynthia*, of all people. It used to be black nearly from head to toe and now it was this. Some things don't suit some people. It just goes with their character.

'Where's your didgereedoo?' Mr Farrelly reminded me of my own Da the way he didn't mind if his kids did anything mad; he just took the piss. Only I never had the guts to push the boat out with my own Da, doing shit like dyeing my hair or anything. Although one Hallowe'en, after I'd made my hair stick up with Coke, Da said – and he was dead serious – that it suited me and that I should keep my hair that way.

'Ha, ha, bloody ha,' said Cynthia. 'I left it in Naas with the bongo drums.'

'Whatever you're into these days. Just as long as you're not doing, y'know . . .' and Mr Farrelly started acting like he was stoned, sucking air between his two fingers pressed up against his lips, crossing his eyes and wobbling his knees around. 'I've heard about you students. Jesus, I just wish you'd warned me on the phone.'

'Hi Cynthia,' I said.

'Ah for Christ's sake Da, it's not as if I shaved my head and got tattoos across my face. It's only clothes.'

'I'm only messing with you, don't jump down my throat. Jeeez! I dunno Jerome. The female constitution! They've no temperament and no sense of humour. That's why they make crap comedians and even worse snooker players.' Mr Farrelly really knew how to wind Cynthia up. 'Have you said hello to Jerome yet?'

'Yeah, I have.'

No she hadn't.

'Right then, let's get out of here. I'm parked on double-yellow lines.'

We were doing the Battle of Vinegar Hill all week. Mr Farrelly had converted his garage and built this extension and turned it into his little playroom. At any one time he'd have a whole train set going or some battle scene from history with all the minute details. To make way for his latest idea he'd either turn his old set into something new or else give the old one to a kids' home or his train club and start from scratch with something else. The whole set-up was mad. You'd always find different stuff in the garage; there were so many little bits and pieces lying around. It was that sort of lived-in mess I always thought I'd like to surround myself with when I'd have my own place. You could just tinker about all day. It reminded me of that kid's bedroom in *ET*. The shelves went up as high as the ceiling with all this deadly gear he'd collected over the years, all that cheapy chip-board wood bulging and looking like it was going to give way with the weight, with Mr Farrelly's trade union badges and this brass eagle and medals he'd collected from different wars all hammered into the side.

His new thing was the 1798 war. I'd told him earlier on in the week that I thought there was a load of old chicken wire in the yard at the back of Da's shop. I thought I'd remembered seeing it maybe a couple of months before and wondered if it would still be there. I went down and it was there all right, after all that time, and Ahmed was laughing saying I'd just beaten the skip they'd ordered for the next Monday, but some of it was rusty, but it didn't matter because there was so much of it, this big roll that I carried up to the Farrellys like the Hunchback of Notre Dame. It was perfect for the job. Chicken wire's the best for moulding into hills and valleys. There was this one huge hump we made and that was going to be Vinegar Hill. We just layered the papier mâché on top. Well, I mixed it and Mr Farrelly layered it. It was his baby. We let this dry for a day and speeded it up with a fan heater, and on the Friday after school I'd started to help him with the paint with all these dark greens and browns. That was the next step, the painting. I was looking forward to the weekend. We were going to finish up the painting and melt the lead and start on the soldiers. Mr Farrelly had moulds for every type of olden-day soldier, even the Irish ones with their sticks called pikes. He'd also bought these to-scale buildings, little plastic ones he was going to paint as stone cottages, and that was going to be Enniscorthy at the bottom of the hill, with the Slaney running through it with cellophane and a mirror.

There was just no way I was going to be able to go out with Cynthia. I was occupied. It was a real team effort; a family effort. Mrs Farrelly kept the food coming and the boys kept the work going like coal into a steam train. All cakes and ham. That was another thing. Mrs Farrelly's cooking. When you're brought up in a family who can't cook or anything and eat tinned food or shit you heat up in a microwave all your life, you really appreciate decent food that's cooked properly, by a woman, sort of. And all this time that I was working away with Mr Farrelly and watching Mrs Farrelly come in and out with food or to have a laugh and me thinking that both of them seemed pretty sound and tuned in and all that because they were quite young, I was thinking how they could have come up with a name like *Cynthia* for their daughter.

I really hated the new crowd. There was just this bunch of cretins who Cynthia was only kind of friendly with in her year when she was still at school, but who she only really got to know over the summer. *I* probably knew them better through the fifth- and sixth-year soccer leagues when we were all mixed up in different teams. Fanger was this dick who was on our team, and to this day I still don't know his full name other than it was Fanning. He was one of these dicks who all the younger lads were really impressed with because he was such a dosser; so sharp in the dressing room and prepared to give it out to the ref. A real dirty shit on the pitch as well – he had those steel studs that were banned in our school. There was him and Richie Traynor and then a couple of their mates who didn't go to our school who Cynthia fell in with. I don't know, I just couldn't get along with them. They were Cynthia's mates, not my mates.

She'd organized with them to go out for the night. She'd had a whole week at college down in Carlow and she still had the energy. I was bollocksed, and I didn't want to – I *couldn't* – go out. Mr Farrelly was all 'Go on out if you want, we can do the modelling some other time', but I didn't want to lose the momentum. I was only just getting into it. I was sort of stuck between two stools – Cynthia was my girlfriend, but I felt I'd be rude if I abandoned all the work. Mr Farrelly was going 'Will you don't be stupid, get out there, go on, go', but fuck, I was tired and I didn't have the cash and it was warm in the house and it was raining outside and it was a half-mile walk to the bus and Cynthia knew I was just making excuses and gave up and said 'Fair enough' and went out and that was it. That was that. That was the last time I ever saw Cynthia.

Most of the night we didn't actually work on the model. Everybody over a certain age is a sucker for *The Late Late Show* and every so often as we were putting on streaks of paint here and there Mr Farrelly would stick his brush in the white spirits and check which guest was on. I'd lost him after the second ad break with some priests doing some debate or some shit.

'You keep an eye on things there Jerome,' he was going. 'Don't do anything too much now. Just top it up a little with the brown while it's still wet. Mix it around, kind of.'

I was looking for the opportunity to be left alone actually because I had my own surprise, my own personal touch. I had this little plastic flag at home that I got sticking out of an ice cream from my Confirmation years ago. It was this American flag, but I peeled the shiny bit off the top of the sticker to leave the rough ripped-up paper bottom underneath and I got out my markers and coloured it in like the tricolour: green and orange with tippex in the middle for the white. I twisted and pushed the flagpole through the top of the hill sort of like it had been planted there by the Irish troops and was sailing in the wind. This was my contribution. *The hill was conquered.* Just to give it that historical detail, that extra bit of reality I'd bet Mr Farrelly hadn't thought of.

I figured he was probably in for the night watching shit on the TV and I'd done all I could on my own with the model, so I popped my head in the door of the living room and said I was off.

'Are you off?' he said to me, and I said I was and I'd be back in the morning and off I went.

It was around six o'clock the next day that I made it around to the Farrellys' gaff again, what with all this fucking backlog of Irish homework that Powell was on my case about getting done. But before lunch I'd been down to the carpet shop again to get this beautiful piece of underlay I'd seen the last day. It was that sort of muck-brown and rough with dimples going all higgledy-piggledy. We could find a use for it along the river-bank or at the bottom of the hill, I was sure.

I knew Mr Farrelly had gone ahead and started melting the lead already because the side window in the garage was open to let the fumes out. I went up and tapped on the glass.

'Jesus, Jerome, you frightened the shit out of me. You popped up there like . . . like fucking . . . I don't know . . . Zig and Zag! Come around to the door.'

I took a look in at the model through the window. He'd been touching the paint up all day. My bits were covered over, although I had to admire the real professional job. I could see it now. The way I painted on the green, it was too bright and colourful like the sun was shining down, like a hill in *The Sound of Music*. When I think of a scene from history I always imagine it with the sun in the sky. Mr Farrelly made it look like it probably properly did. All dulled as if it had been raining and a million feet and wooden wheels had trampled on the ground. He'd taken the flag off as well. I forgot. The English won that one.

Mr Farrelly wasn't really acting himself. He just stood in the doorway with his feet see-sawing up and down on the metal saddle and his hand jigging around with the chain. Usually he'd open the door and I'd walk in no problem. I wouldn't have to wait for permission or anything. But he was just standing at the doorway talking to me like I'm the milkman or someone. Something was going on in his head.

'Mr Farrelly, I've got some new stuff for you. Stuff I think we could use for the new model,' I was saying.

'Ah grand, good. What is it there?'

'It's just some old scraps I got from the carpet shop, y'know, the one where my Da used to work . . .'

'Ah yeah, I do, yeah.'

'They were gonna chuck it all out. It's just loose cuttings. I think we could make it into a riverbank. Sort of curve it round and glue on goldfish gravel or something.'

'Ah right. Right. Good idea. Well. I don't know now. I think we had everything that we needed, y'know? But leave it here anyway, I'll have a look and see what's what. Look, Jerome . . .'

'It might make a good base for something else maybe though. It's a good muck colour. I was thinking maybe the Battle of the Somme.' I hadn't actually thought of the Battle of the Somme before; it just came to me then.

'All right so . . . Listen, Jerome . . . Look . . .'

All these ideas were flying into my mind, all these deadly artistic ideas.

'I was thinking maybe we could even make trenches in it by sticking it down to some of those oasis flower blocks and gouging out grooves.'

'. . . Look.' Mr Farrelly stopped. 'You're a good lad and, y'know, you've got your whole life ahead of you . . . and there's other y'know, *different* – things, horizons . . .'

He was becoming a bit edgy. I wasn't getting this. I was all scratching my face and shuffling around looking down at the ground.

'What I'm trying to say is . . . Actually listen. Just come on inside. We'll get tea.'

So basically what Mr Farrelly was trying to say after tea and biscuits and a sit-down around the table and two minutes of talking about the weather and football and shit, was that Cynthia had had a chat with him some time that morning – and I think she'd probably done the dirt on me during the night – about me. About me and her and the way things were going. She was sort of fed up. She wanted to find a way of telling me that she wanted to end it and couldn't think of one and ended up crying and going all hysterical in her Da's arms and Mr Farrelly said he'd do the talking, the poor shit. But that was all. It wasn't as if I wasn't expecting it or anything.

'So I'll leave all these scraps here with you and you can see what to make of them,' I said as I was going for the door.

'Okay. All right,' said Mr Farrelly getting up from his seat. 'Ah, you're a grand lad, Jerome. A grand lad. I'll let you out there . . .'

And that was the last time I saw Cynthia's Da, except for that one time he was in a rush down at the Spar buying a load of briquettes before that match started that time.

'. . . A grand lad.'

FIVE

'So you're a single man again,' says Gary, and I said, 'Yeah', but it was strange because the lighter I'd only bought fucking forty-five minutes before wasn't working, and he goes 'Back on the hunt' and I went 'Yeah', and I was flicking and flicking the thing, and I knew it wasn't the gas because the top went *tsss* when I pressed the button, and he's all 'A world of possibilties' and shit and I was 'Yeah, yeah', and it was the fucking flint was banjaxed, so I said, 'To hell with this anyway', and went back down to the shops to get a new lighter and for the walk.

But yeah. Who knows, I was thinking.

The lighter magically starts working just outside the shop, but I thought I'd keep quiet about it. I could see it was Brian Waters' brother on tonight behind the till. With anyone else on in the shop, I might have turned back, but I thought I could have a go at Brian Waters' brother. He was putting boxes of yellow Bic pens up in a stack behind him. I slapped the lighter on the counter and then I started tapping it fast and repeatedly until I'd got his attention. I went on about how he'd sold me damaged goods and how it just wasn't on, and then I told him that his head looked like the top of a whistle on an old steam locomotive train and I asked him had anyone ever told him that before. There was a big green card hanging up with lines of small locks that were for sale hanging off it, and it just would have been perfect to rip the card off its Blu Tac and throw it down in a rage. I wished everyone in the world was like Brian Waters' brother, because he was the kind of person that made all your talk sound sharp, like something from a film script. If you were talking to him you could say what you liked and you had the confidence to control the way the air came out of your lungs as you spoke so that you could give the words the right effect. You get the feeling sometimes that after watching hours of TV you'll be able to go out and talk in ideal dialogue, and you often don't, but sometimes you do, and Brian Waters' brother was one of the few people I'd ever met where you could. He was one of those who'd just *let* you read the magazines without saying anything.

'All right Mark,' I said to him as I took a copy of *Empire* down off the shelf.

'All right,' he says to me all nervous.

People were coming in and out of the shop to buy crisps for soakage before going into The Tankard, our local. People were coming and going, and they didn't bother me, half or most of the fucks don't bother me, but there was something about this time when the door swung open. You know the way it is sometimes, when your head is bowed and you're reading the magazines, but you sense something off to the side, as if a CCTV camera is attached to your head.

This girl who came in, I really fancied her, even while I was going out with Cynthia. I hardly ever saw her around although I knew she lived in the area. One time I got off the bus in town after I'd caught her walking down the street. I don't

know what came over me. It was three stops away from where
I was meant to be getting off. It was impulse. I'd seen her on
the street and I just jumped up and hit the bell. I felt like a
dick the second I stepped onto the path. I didn't think she saw
me and I ducked into a shop. Then I waited there until my
heart calmed down. It wasn't just the look of her. It was the
kind of life she seemed to have. There was just something
there that seemed all exotic. Her mates and that.

I couldn't see her mates when she went back out to join
them; there was too much shine on the glass. I went up closer
to the window to get a clearer look, but they were crossing the
road and huddled over, and they were heading for The
Tankard. This was a real revelation. This girl wasn't the sort I'd
have thought would have been part of The Tankard crowd.
There was me half-keeping an eye out for her all the time, and
her never seeming to be in the area because I thought she was
a town person, more ambitious, and here she was going into
The Tankard. It almost felt like a trap, drawing me in there.
But the effect she had on me, whenever I saw her. She filled
me up with something. She was the kind of girl you'd bend
over in the dark at home over and clench your fists and cry
about.

While I was going out with Cynthia I'd tried to avoid social-
izing in my area. We only really went drinking in town.
There's something about The Tankard; the atmosphere or
something.

Everyone hates the owner, Sid Byrne, so I'm not the only one
there. He ruined the name and the effect. All the old lads in the
area knew the pub as The Tankard, but when Sid Byrne bought

it and ran it with his son Lou, they changed it to Byrne's Tankard, which doesn't have the same ring. They took down the old wooden sign and put up this thing with a plastic glaze.

Thtrawberry Thid. He's got this wicked lisp. 'Thing a thong of thickthpenth, Thid!' Part of his palate is missing. He had an operation. He's such a dick. He's always getting people barred for fuck-all reason. It's a *pub*! Folks are *going* to get pissed and they're *going* to fall around the place and they're *going* to cause trouble.

But it's the people as well, I won't kid myself. I don't like that crowd down there. It's a real no-go zone on weekends.

I was looking for some crowd to go in on the tail of. I didn't want to be noticed. I don't know, you imagine sometimes in pubs you'll walk in and the juke box will stop and everyone will look up. Then I thought I was overestimating the effect I have. Nobody would be bothered with me, even the people I'd know from school. The rest of the crowd I'd be too far removed from.

I took a stool by this ledge that goes along the back of a partition that divides an area of seats from this space that leads to a side door. Somebody had left a pint unfinished there, so I pretended it was mine. I didn't want to go up to the bar yet. I wanted to sit and think about what I'd be doing, about what I'd say. I looked around to see could I see the girl.

The Tankard was the same old dive as I remembered it. It was filling up pretty steadily with all these characters from the neighbourhood who I only saw once a year, usually at Christmas mass. I used to wonder where all these people hid during the other 360-odd days. It was hard to imagine there

could be so many young people in my area. There seemed to
be this whole new crowd of teens. I could remember other
stuff the couple of times I had been in The Tankard: the Child
of Prague up above the spirits with the wax face that had
melted; that Inter-Pub Pool League fixtures table up on the
wall from way back; that really gay picture of the chef pointing to the restaurant upstairs saying, 'Eat, Drink and Be
Merry'. But I didn't recognize any of these new young people.
I hadn't even noticed them around the place growing up. You'd
think you would.

I spotted Father Vesey hanging around on his own, this
reject priest in our school that they couldn't find a proper job
for. He was one of the few leftovers from when all the normal
teachers came in and the priests died out, but he was hardly
ever in the school any more. He was hidden away in the
priests' home mainly these days. He used to do shit like civics
and home economics and the school masses. We had him for
civics one year. People used to take the piss out of him, but I
found him quite interesting sometimes. He'd been a young
padre with the Irish army in the Congo back in the sixties.
He'd got this bad reputation in the school for showing some
class a wound on the top of his leg that he got from an operation to get rid of an infected mosquito bite. He'd started to
roll the leg of his trouser up, and he was going, 'See that there
now; ah feck it!' and the material wouldn't go up beyond the
knobble in his knee, so then he unzipped his fly. All the girls
sort of liked him, although they said he was a bit of a lecher.
Father Sleazy. Even some of the fellas had stories about him.
He wasn't the kind of guy you'd want to get talking to in
front of other people. People used to guess what his real name

was, and they came up with all sorts of weird things, and then it turned out that his name was fucking Piet, like a Dutchman.

I did another survey of the lounge. It was a big old room and it was pretty near full. I was in as good a position as there was to see everything, but it was difficult. I kept on seeing movement here and there that I thought was the girl through groups of other people. Then I spotted her around near the cigarette machine. She was on the other side of the lounge, but a gap had opened up for a second through the crowd and I saw her quickly.

That impulse I'd felt on the bus that time took me over again; *vwum vwum, vwum vwum.* I slid off the stool and made my way through the people sort of bent over. Then I straightened up and strode towards her. When I straightened up I seemed so much taller than everyone else. I shot up above everyone's shoulders. I stopped and looked around. It seemed like I could even see above the bluey smoke pall. I could see it rising and then bedding in at a point. When I got closer to the girl I felt my breath quiver as I breathed out. It kind of came out in a chopped-up wave. This was ridiculous. What is she going to think I am, I thought. I veered off and went to the bar to get a drink. Maybe if I had a bit of bolstering I'd get my head together.

Sid Byrne was behind the bar. I tried to think of a drink with loads of S's in it but nothing was coming into my head.

'*Now!*' The cunt always shouted at you. 'Yourthelf?'

I saw this black bottle hanging up. The stuff in it looked black as well. I thought I'd try something different. 'What's that liquorice stuff?'

'What are you talking about? Don't wathte my time. *Lou!*

You look after thith chap.' He shouted out 'chap' like he was talking about the chaps on your hands. He hated anyone under the age of twenty.

'What's the liquorice stuff in the bottle up there?' I asked the son.

'Liquorice? There's no such a thing. Eh . . . There's sambuca though. You probably mean *this*. This is aniseed, not liquorice.'

'I'll have a . . . whatever . . . of sambuca then. A measure or a short or a squirt or a glass or a pint or whatever,' I said. 'Aniseed? Hm. Like Black Jacks.'

He didn't respond as he poured the glass. It came out all see-through. I bet his Da never allowed him sweets as a kid, I said to myself.

'Is it a strong drink?' I asked him again.

'I don't know. I don't care.'

'Is that a collection box on the counter?'

'Yeah.'

'What's it for?'

'Dunno.'

'Is it busier here on Fridays or Saturdays?'

'Dunno.'

'When are you going to take that pool-league thing down? I mean, maybe you're still doing the pool league, I don't know, but that thing's been up since the eighties, so when are you going to take it down?'

'Fucking Christ,' he went under his breath.

'Your Da's a faggot,' I blurted out.

'Listen here, you little . . . *queer*. Go and fuck off. Pay up and fuck off.'

I paid up but I didn't go. I should have. Father Vesey had spotted me. He'd made eye contact with me and he was honing in.

'Sam-buc-a! Oh how very *tropical* Master Morris!'

He turned his back to the bar and propped his elbows up and sidled up beside me.

'I must correct myself, of course. Sambuca is an Italian drink and Italy isn't in the tropics. So you couldn't call it tropical then. I suppose it's *Mediterranean*.' He was doing that chesty old person's laugh to himself. 'It's just that saying "that's a very *Mediterranean* drink" sounds so . . .' he stopped and looks around left and right and whispers '. . . *feckin'* stupid!'

I hate it the way teachers and shit feel they have to do that. Drop in bad language to make them sound all young and in touch.

'Ah, yes. Tropical and Mediterranean climes. I used to be a geography teacher, did you know that?'

I shook my head. I lashed back the sambuca. It had a weird smell that hit your nose from the back. It sort of gave off fumes.

'I did. And not a lot of people know *this*, but I have a degree in geology. That's *rocks* to the man on the street. Hm. UCD. I was a geography teacher for years. I taught English too. But you know what?'

I didn't answer. I was looking around the lounge. This was so embarrassing. People might have thought I was being molested.

'I gave it all up to teach Irish. Yes!' He hushed his voice again. '*Yes*.'

I knew he was drawing attention to me. He was swinging his hands too much.

'I'd *die* for that language. That's no exaggeration. I *love* that language. But they made me give that up too.'

He wasn't drinking anything out of his glass. He was swilling the drink around to help him make his points. Loads of it was spilling. 'It's *Jerome*, isn't it, your first name?'

'It is, yeah. Jerome Morris.'

'I thought so. It was either Jerome or Jarlath in my head. You know, I knew it was a *Galway* name.'

I'd managed to order in another pint through all this, from this other barman on duty.

'It took a second to register when I saw you, but I got there in the end,' Father Vesey went on. 'I'm quite good with names and I'm all right with faces, but never at the same time! It's just so hard to put a name to a face when you're not used to seeing that particular face in a certain context, you know what I mean? The Jerome Morris I'd be familiar with now is the Jerome Morris who used to sit quietly in civics class, the one who'd always gone ahead at least a chapter in advance in his reading of – what was it? – *I Am David*. The one who I'd always marked down as a worrier. Heh. You're still a worrier, aren't you Jerome? I can see it in your fidgeting. Fidget fingers. I couldn't help notice. I still look out for my past students, you see. You were a bit quiet sitting over there. *Taciturn*. I have a keen eye for body language. I have faculties in my brain which can decipher these things. I'd always had you down as a worrier. *Over*-preparedness. I'd you marked down above all the other boys and on a par with some of the girls as a *worrier*.'

The girl was hovering around the bar pretty close by. She

wafted by me on her way to the bogs. I breathed in and held my breath to trap the scent in my lungs. I got another drink.

'I'll tell you something Jerome, that *I Am David* lark, that was all a ruse, you know that? I had no real regard for it, or other people's fiction generally, English-language fiction. Books are books, words on paper, people chancing their arm as they go along. It's all just random thoughts, strung together and made to look coherent by a good editor, that's all. You think there was a message in all that? Ha. No. Well. There probably was, but it was secondary to what I was aiming for. *Poetry*, now that requires *real* discipline, cadence, meter, carefully thought-out ideas. But books . . . no. No. I never *expected* lads and girls of twelve, thirteen, fourteen to take to these readings. It was all a ploy, a little sort of . . . *testing the water*, a little bit of character assessment. That's what civics was all about. To me, now. Remember when I'd ask each student how far they'd read up to? Remember? I'd go up to each pupil and ask them quietly, individually? The ones who'd raced ahead – *they* were the ones to look out for. When I'd say, "Read up to the third chapter for the next day", I'd *mean* the third chapter, not the fourth chapter, or the seventh chapter or the tenth chapter. These are the ones who's futures I'd be concerned about. Genuinely, now. Even the students I have at the moment. The lads who'd shoulder you in the corridor, give a bit of stick, all right – *chancers* – the lot; but *these*, these are the people who make it. *These* are the people who have the balls and the chutzpah to make it up to the top in the banks or the supermarkets or the wherever. You know? You need to start looking people in the eyes more Jerome.'

Father Vesey eyed the drink in his hand. 'It's all coming out now, isn't it? Huh? Heh, heh, heh. Tricks of the trade. I'll tell you what though. It's good to see you out and about. It's good to see you out . . .' the voice hushed again and he glanced all frantic from side to side '. . . *pissed as a hoor!* Heh, heh, heh.'

Father Vesey's laughs trailed off into a grumble. There was one of those silences you get after people have stopped making a point and you sense that they don't know what to say next, almost like they've run out of steam. I'll say something, anything, to break those silences even if it means keeping a shitty conversation going. I tried to recall something Father Vesey might have said to us in civics class, but I was finding it hard to think. Those classes just passed me by. Then I remembered vaguely this time he was going on feeling all sorry for himself saying he never really wanted to be a priest to begin with, that his parents and even his brother pushed him into doing it, and he got trapped in the seminary, and eventually he just grew into the job.

'I suppose, what you're saying then,' I said, 'is that if you have the opportunity to just . . . *go for it* in life, it's a shame not to.'

'Very true.'

'I mean, say *you*, for instance; you could have had all these ambitions growing up, but you couldn't do anything with them because you'd joined the priesthood, and everything you might have wanted to do was limited by that.'

'Very true,' he said. 'Like I said, I was a geography teacher, and I've always had a tremendous interest in travelling, and I always as a young lad had the idea of just going off and seeing the world. And after I came back from Africa with the army I thought, well, this isn't looking too bad, maybe there's more to this vocation. But of course, I ended up just getting shunted around from parish to parish in the Dublin diocese. All a bit of a come-down. But then, in the religious you see, they talk about this thing, sublimation, and once you learn how to regulate one type of energy with sublimation, you can use it in other ways. I channelled my wanderlust into taking an interest in whatever parish I was sent, getting to know all the little nooks and crannies, all of the people. In Donabate. In Ballyfermot. Glencree. Harold's Cross. Irishtown. Wherever the archbishop sent me.'

I went through in my head the places he said – Donabate, Ballyfermot, Glencree, Harold's Cross. *Harold's Cross.*

'I don't know. You're a grand lad though. You'll be all right,' Father Vesey went on. 'How's life at home Jerome? Your father passed away this year, isn't that right?'

'Everything's okay. It's grand. We're getting along. When were you sent to Harold's Cross?'

'Oh, eh, late seventies, early eighties, something . . . It can't be easy though. Must be tough.'

'No, it's all right really. The early eighties?'

'And who's there at home? There's that older brother – what is it – Garret? Gary? – the athlete – and your mother. How's your poor mother been through all this? Is she coping okay?'

'My Mother. Yes. I don't know.'

This bird, fucking hell. It was like, a single touch, just a tap, and *zing!* On her way past me again I bent my knee out a bit to get a rub. It was like one of those divining rods for water. My leg just twisted around and followed the source. Even though I was wearing jeans and she was wearing cords it felt like a piece of silk or mohair or a smooth bar of soap running over my skin.

I caught the glint off the side of her cheek. She had a trace of green glitter stuck on. I love that; I love the way girls do that, when they glam up. I thought I'd catch her glance. She was showing me an open face. I turned quickly but I made it too obvious. I was stuck and I was just staring at her.

Her face was turned away again slightly. I could see now she was following the gaze of her mates. They were staring at me. It was now *really* obvious. I didn't recognize her mates except for one. The birds were pretty much all rides. One of the blokes with them was Roly Shaw. She turned to trace the stares.

'Do I know you?'

My jawbone stayed fixed but the top of my head sort of flipped back. My mouth was open in a real goofy way. I knew they could probably see right in. I had to say something but no words came out. There was just this loud hot rasp which tasted of drink and aniseed.

'Look. Do I know you?'

'What's your name?' I got out eventually.

'Carmel. *Do I know you?*'

'Caramel.'

'Do I fucking know you?'

'Cream caramel.'

Roly Shaw comes over and he eyeballs me. 'Listen mate, I don't wanna hurt you 'cause I don't wanna cause a scene and everything, but you're only gonna get this one warning.' I felt a knuckle press hard in my ribs.

The group of them just shifted, lock stock. Fair play to Roly. He didn't want any hassle. He'd been taken in by this girl like I was. It was just so silly, I was thinking. The way girls can take a hold on you like that.

I went around to the other side of the bar where it joins the hatch into the main pub. I saw Father Sleazy down the other end. The stupid Walter Mitty fuck. He'd nabbed some other poor dick. I don't know though, maybe I could get him some other time when he's sober and not over-excited, I thought. Get some information out of him. I got myself another drink before I left. I sucked it and suckled at it, twirled the head around with my tongue, wrapped my lips around the rim of the glass, breathed air into it, lifted it and swallowed it really quickly.

3

SIX

Something weird happens to metal in the cold. That's why your tongue sticks to bars on swings and slides if you lick them when it's all icy. The gates on our estate go *ping!* if you bang them. Engines just seize up. Gary's car was dying on him. It was one of those freezing mornings, the first day after the summer when you get frost that always happens around the end of November, or some time after the spiders come in, but before the trees are completely bare. He'd got himself this old Datsun for two or three hundred quid. A *Datsun*, like. It wasn't even a Nissan it was so old – 78 D. Datsun changed their name to Nissan in nineteen eighty something. I mean, I don't know anything about the names of cars and what's a good one and what's a bad one but you could tell this was a total tin can heap of shit. It was making a noise like a fart on a bench at mass and then just dying off. *Phut phut g-r-r-r-r.*

I was having my own problems with machines myself. The door of the cooker was literally *hanging* off. For my breakfast lately I'd been going through this real phase. They were these things, these bagels you cooked. Not the ones you'd buy coming in the door of the garage that got all the lead poisoning and you did in the toaster, although it started off with those. It was the ones you got in a box, frozen, with tomato and meat on top, the ones you'd have to heat up in the cooker. It was a real pain in the hole not being able to do them in the microwave because I'd be in a rush for school in the mornings, but they were pretty nice so I'd persevere. I'd have that and then this rock sugar shit for energy. But I'd got into the habit of leaning on the cooker door, leaving it open while I watched that my breakfast wasn't burning. It was over-abuse. It gave in and the hinge just went.

I didn't want Gary to think I was some spa. I taped the door on the left-side with lino tape. It was all right. I mean, stop-gap and all, but the tape was that brown colour of the cooker and you wouldn't notice.

Jesus though, I had this name or number in my head. It was flashing around and then it was gone: the guy who came around and fixed the cooker and the fan and all that before. He went on about if you had problems or shit again just give him a buzz, the number was on the card, the man for the job, look no further. I *knew*, I'd let him in the last time, the only one in the house. I knew it was somewhere. Somewhere around in a cup or somewhere. I'd seen it recently. Shit. I really wanted to have all this tied up before Gary caught on I was a real spa case.

'Operation fucking shit-arse Datsun. Call the fucking . . . John . . . Hannibal Smith.' Gary was coming in for another kettle of water. His work wasn't until half ten but he wanted to heat the engine up or melt the ice on the windscreen to have it ready on time. It was his first car. He couldn't keep away from the thing. First bit of light in the morning, crack of dawn, *bang*, polish job or a tyre check or his dick up the exhaust pipe or whatever. It was handy though for work and

Gary suddenly got this knack for engines like he was born with it.

They were the two big things Gary had done recently, the car and the job. He'd got this job in an office in town for a couple of hours a day. A friend of a friend of a friend sort of thing. He'd kept his contacts back home even though he'd been away in America. It was an extra few quid.

He was in a money mood this morning. I hated that. It just wasn't something that interested me. It was Gary's responsibility, that. He was the older one. He was like, 'I want to have a word with you about the finances before you head off for school', and then he reeled off all this bollocks about the money situation. He might as well have been going 'Blahblahblah.' I wasn't listening. The words were skimming over my head like my brain was in a bag from the butcher's. I just picked a knot on the wooden spoon hanging up on the rack on the table and fixed my eyes on it and went into a daze, going, 'Yeah, right, yeah' every couple of seconds to let on I was paying attention.

'. . . So it's yours there to use, but don't go mad with it.' I caught just at the end. 'Now. I'll give this fucker one last go and if I don't get a result I'm gonna buy my bike back off Kenny Digges' son.' You always pick up the shit that isn't important.

I fancied another cup of tea before heading off for school. All that caffeine got you through the first two classes before little break and then you were on cruise control. But you need to drink a pot and then eat the slops at the bottom to really get that sort of buzz, I find. Somebody in America *died* from injecting caffeine directly into their veins.

But shit, shit, shit, I forgot, Gary had the kettle out with the car. I looked out the window. The bonnet was up and he was fiddling around. How could anyone know what they were doing with that mess; all those tubes and wires and shit? I didn't feel like going out to get the kettle back. I'd had enough bollocks for one morning. There'd been too much talk.

This thing wafted into my head. *The old radio, the old radio.* We have this old radio that we took the insides out of and clicked back together again. We use it as a secret money box for phone bills and the ESB. The one before was really obvious – this clay frog that was smashed into and the money was nicked when the knackers broke in. Gary must have been talking about it and it just lodged in my head without me noticing. I went over and pulled the two halves apart. There was this big wad of notes. I went through them. Twenty, thirty, fifty, seventy . . . around a hundred quid. A hundred and ten quid. I was sure he'd been saying that this was the emergency stash for special savings. Still. Handy, I was thinking. I left for school through the back door and hopped over the wall into the Bents' side passage and out their driveway because I didn't want to have to talk to Gary.

School was okay around then. I was just left alone. Left alone to daze. I think the teachers had given up on me. I'd gone past the 'three warnings and you're out' stage. Actually, I'd gone past that a long while before. I'd always be getting into shit for falling asleep. It was getting like a routine for the teachers. There were the mad-bastard dossers and the people who wouldn't shut up and the you'd-forget-your-head-if-it-wasn't-screwed-on types and I was in this other category. Just this dozy shit. I was always getting these warnings. Now they didn't even dare give me one warning. I'm not one to look for sympathy, but it can be useful sometimes. They probably thought I'd bawl out crying if I was given out to, because of Da. I wouldn't have given a shit. I mean, I would just have *taken it*. Big fucking deal. I was allowed sit by the window and just stare and I was left alone.

It was kind of funny because I'd notice the teachers staring at me but they wouldn't give out. They'd have to catch themselves before they snapped and started going, 'What the divel's going on with ya now Master Morris, wha, wha?' They'd have to tell themselves that here was a special case. Nobody asked me questions because they were afraid I'd get them wrong. They thought it might still be a delicate situation. I mean, it *wasn't*, but it must have been difficult being a teacher in that sort of position. Christ, it sounds like I felt sorry for them. I *didn't*. I didn't at all, especially Mr Powell. Powell was gas. He hated me totally. Always did, since first year, and it's an ambition of mine to piss on his grave. He'd do his classes all the time from the back of the classroom, leaning up against the wall going on with all his *as Gaeilge tá mé ag dul blahblahblah* shite. But I could sense him behind, breathing down my *fucking* neck when he was quiet or when he'd slur his words like he was distracted about something, sizing up whether the time was right to lay into me yet, whether the mourning period was over.

He had ways of getting at me though. I hadn't been doing my homework. He'd suddenly introduced this penalty-points system – *suddenly* – and you'd pick up *dearg* and *buí* cards for not doing work or for messing and you'd build up these points and these would be taken out on you at the end of the term through detention. The whole system was set up to get at *me*. It was no coincidence. By the end of the term it would have been okay to give out shit, and grind the little toss-pot into the ground again, and rip me to shreds, that was his thinking. It was like that saying, 'Points mean prizes', except points meant fucking pent-up fucking anger to Powell.

He totally ruined my best subject too. I was *good* at religion. I mean, I hardly ever spoke up in class or anything, but I could understand it. I could follow the videos and the debates. I actually enjoyed it. All talking about drugs and the Third World. But we got Powell for religion in fifth and sixth year. We had him for pass Irish as well, but the religion was ridiculous. He actually gave us religion *homework*. He was actually going to set a religion *exam*. He started to teach us shit like shit out of the Bible and we went back to those *oh holy holy* Veritas books. He gave one go of the video and that was it. Nobody took it seriously. It was this American film, *My Race-hate Mom*, about the Ku Klux Klan and about how you have to make your own decisions in life, about how your destiny is in your own hands. It was so old and crap and hilarious. So *seventies*. Everyone was cracking their shites. Powell just lost his top, he flipped out completely. And when he got angry his West Brit accent would come through really strong. It was like the charge of the Light Brigade or chasing the Nazis around the desert. *Stand up guards . . . Make ready . . . Aim . . . Fiy-yah!* He was this funny mix. Born a Protestant but converted into a Catholic. He totally threw himself into the whole Catholic thing and being into Irish and Cúchulainn; all that. It was like he was trying to make up for lost time by being a Protestant for forty years. It really got to him the way he couldn't find a proper Irish translation for his name, you could tell. But you can't teach an old dog new tricks they say. That's what the sixth years last year were saying after their retreat. Every year the sixth years go on their retreat down to Powell's place down in Wexford and now it was coming up to our turn. He had this old castle down there that had been in his family for hundreds of years, all covered in ivy with crows flying around. There were 50 acres of land around it, and you'd go down and sit around at the top of the tower and point at things and talk about God. He let on that he was this total 'Ra-head and, in fact, you could imagine him if there was a war down there buying in loads of guns and hiding people in his castle like Roger Casement, but the sixth years last year were saying that he acted like the royal family and that the locals *treated* him like the royal family, all mowing his lawns and doing his gardening. They were saying he probably had one of those old guns with sort of a trumpet on the barrel and he'd just pick off culchies from his tower like in *Schindler's List*. And okay, that was probably a load of shite, like the story of him doing black magic down in the cellar, but – and as much as I hated the cunt – I still wanted to go down and check it all out. I mean, it was different from your usual retreat set-up, lying around on your back on the floor listening to tapes of the ocean or pretending you were this girl going into labour. I don't know, I sort of assumed it would be free though, but apparently this was all part of a big side-project Powell had been doing, these retreat groups he'd been running for all different schools and not just ours, so it was going to cost us the standard price of fifteen quid each. I just wasn't sure yet whether I'd be able to come up with that sort of cash. My

Banklink from the summer was already getting down to zero and I was relying on there just being money around the house from Gary and shit.

I don't know why now but I'd been forcing myself into the habit of staying in for lunch. I suppose it would have been too easy to go home and mope around the house, so I figured, 'Toughen up, sunshine.' The yard and the field though. Just walking around would make you depressed. I was eating my lunch in the bunker and then I went for a walk around the yard and the field and it would make you depressed, really. Our school seemed to pull in all the people from the local area, so 90 per cent or whatever would go home at lunch. They'd all just flood home. It was like that 'We don't need no education' video.

The whole place was a prison at lunchtime, sort of bleak and deserted. Looking at the yard, it was like one of those old prison yards in films with the walls of four buildings around the sides. There was even this light fall of snow like in images of prisons you think of in your head, although it was that Irish snow with rain mixed in that wouldn't stick to the ground. But I wasn't excited about it even a bit. Usually snow brought out this natural reaction in me, as if I was a little kid again, but now I felt I was walking around with chains on my ankles like I was looking up to the sky for a splinter of light, free light, from a prison.

Then I turned off by the gym into the field and it was even more depressing. Little groups of people here and there – girls and boys, boys and girls – all huddled together, all miles apart in the field, and each group you could tell what they were into just by their jackets and by the way they stood and by the way they spat. You could point to each group and say, 'Right, you're into football; you're into fucking shit; you're into more fucking shit; you're into this and that; you're into whatever.' *I'm* the dick though. Here's me thinking all this, and then feeling an even bigger dick just walking around on my own. I looked around like I had one of those gun-sights painted on my eyeballs, this big red electronic target, just picking people off like Powell with the culchies with his gun. I was thinking too about this retreat and where I'd get the money from. I'd look forward to it if I knew I could pay for it.

This kid – this bloke – from first year by the looks of it, comes up to me and he asks for a light, no qualms or anything. Three different reactions, all one after the other, came into my head, *pop, pop, pop.* First, I was thinking, 'Who the fuck do you think you are you cocky little shit?' And then I thought, 'Well hang on, say if that was me in first year and I wanted a smoke', and even though I'd never have gone up to a sixth year for a light I was thinking, 'That bloke's got a bit of something I wish I'd had when I was younger' and I thought, 'All right so' and gave him a light and that was that. But then I was thinking as he fucks off back to his dickhead mates like he's fucking Bruce Willis or something, 'He's too cocky for his age, he needs to be taken down a peg or two', and I wished I'd burst his lip just to show him what life's all about.

The whole sympathy thing *is* handy though. I was getting pissed off with the idea of just hanging around for another half-hour crunching my feet around in the frost. I was looking even less forward to another three classes.

It might look like a prison but at least you can walk straight out the gates if you want. So I just breezed out, right past the teachers' canteen.

The priests' home is across the road from the school. It has grilles over the windows because these kids threw rocks at the glass once and it got broken into a couple of times before. You wouldn't be able to get to it unless you left the school grounds, and if you did you'd be breaking the rules because the rules say you either stay in the grounds or go straight home for lunch. But now I was on my way home for good, and no one else was around, so I thought, 'Now's the time.' I'd been meaning to drop in before but I only would have been able before or after school, and someone might have seen me then and made some insinuation about me. But now this was the chance.

This really ancient priest answers the door. He had a hearing aid in and he looked down at me over a pair of reading glasses.

'I'm looking for Father Vesey,' I said. 'Father Piet Vesey. Is he around?'

The priest didn't answer.

'I'm a student in the school. I'm here to see him for a reason.'

It was like it was taking a second for me to register with him.

'Oh sorry, yes. Father Vesey's just on the phone at the moment, but if you'd like to come in and wait . . .'

I took a step inside the porch. Then I thought for a second.

'Actually, it's all right. It's not that important.'

'He won't be a second. Sure you might as well come on in.'

'Nah, it's okay. I'm in a hurry. I'll catch him some other time.'

I wasn't really prepared. This visit was only a real spur-of-the-moment thing, and I wasn't really prepared. I'd get him another time, I thought.

I continued on my way home and I got in and just rang up our headmaster, The Taoiseach, going, 'Uugh, I don't feel too good sir, I think I better stay home for the rest of the day.' And The Taoiseach's going, 'Don't worry about that Jerome, whatever's the best for you, go easy on yourself. I'll tell the teachers.'

There's this thing. I don't know why I took it out again to look at. It's a bit gay actually. It's this woollen cushion cover done up in blue and yellow with 'JEROME' all knitted across in different colours. There used to be a cushion inside it. They weren't sure who sent it to them in the convent – it was just sent in the post, no names or numbers, or anything – and then it was passed on to our house. You don't have to be Inspector Gadget though. I used to think how come my Ma knew my name was Jerome, but, apparently, so Da told me later, she left a note with the pram saying, 'Please take care of my Jerome.' So she was the one who thought up the name first, and I was stuck with it because you can't change the name of a baby after a certain amount of weeks. It's like with dogs, you learn to respond to a name and the parents have to go with that even if it's shit. It's like, if I'd been caught nicking a biscuit in a jar when I was a baby, the only name that would have made me stop nicking the biscuit after a certain amount of time would have been Jerome. I wish I'd been called something different though. Or I wish Da had just gone for another name anyway and drilled it into my head and made me learn it. Jerome, like; I hate that name. It's embarrassing. It's too weird. I've never met anyone else with it except for this old teacher who'd retired but kept on coming back to our school for this Lenten appeal shit. I would do what some people do and use my middle name, but my middle name's worse. I'm not going to say it because it's even more embarrassing.

It's Frances. With an 'e'. F-R-A-N-C-*E*-S. They fucked up on the birth cert. Da said it was just student nurses, that they're all thick.

It was only when I saw the note on the cooker door that the thing came back to me. I mean, my blood was *really* boiling. Gary the fucker had put this note on the cooker saying not to touch it because he'd found this spare part for the hinge and he hadn't time to fix it before work so I was to leave it till he got home. And right then I remembered where the cooker man's business card was, right *THEN!* It was in this plastic picnic cup in the press under the sink where we kept washers and nuts. I should have remembered it from the last time. I should have remembered it and then there'd have been none of this bullshit about Gary being better than me. If I just could have got the guy around for repairs before I'd left in the morning then it would have been all settled and there wouldn't have been all this 'I'm the man of the house' bullshit from Gary.

And when my blood's boiling I'll fucking go at it. Whatever needs to be done, I'll go at it. I'll fucking tackle the shit. I wasn't going to stand by like some faggot.

I pulled the door down again to check out the damage. I'd need to unscrew the other hinge and take the whole door off and then try to find this other bit Gary was going on about and put everything back on again. The thing was, you couldn't get at the head of the screw to loosen it. It was turned towards the frame of the door. It couldn't be done; it wasn't like a proper screw. I needed to sort of turn the door and twist it and twist it. Just keep on twisting it until it snapped, twisting and twisting. The only way you could take the door off would be to break the other hinge and if there were spare parts for one hinge then there'd be spare parts for the other, I was sure. And then it was like, '*Raaaaargh*'; Hulk Hogan. It was like, '*Ladies and Gentlemen, the super-heavyweight champion of the world, Mr Jerome Morris!*' I could feel the veins on my neck almost explode and the metal just snapped and before I knew it I was pissed off and my foot had kicked the glass out of the door and the frame was lying on the floor, battered into this weird shape, like that thing, a rhombus. But I'd calmed down by the time Gary came back home from work.

Gary was sound about it. He didn't freak out or anything with the damage. And that's a good thing, I suppose. He was, 'Okay, so what happened here?', and I told him that the door just must have fallen down with its own weight and twisted the other hinge and smashed on the ground. So everything was cool. It was like that thing that French teacher said. In first year we had this student French teacher who was going on about how important the French language was because of all the words that the French had given to the English language. She was going on with this, 'Oooh, well there's "café" and "restaurant"', and then she comes out with this other thing that no one had heard, this 'sang froid' word and she explained that it was someone who's able to keep their composure and stay calm. That's what Gary has. He kind of calculates every-thing and takes it in his stride. He finds humour in situations.

'Gremlins,' he was going.

'What?'

'Gremlins. Those yokes that get into machines and fuck them up. They've spread from the car to the cooker, that's what they've done. Everything just seems to be falling apart at the same time.'

'Yeah. I know. I'm sorry.'

'Jesus, don't be saying *sorry*. Shit happens. It's not your fault. When you're down you're down, Jer. You're on the ground and someone kicks you in the bollocks and everything happens at once.'

I couldn't work Gary out sometimes. He was just *accepting* my answer. I was going mental a few hours before; Gary was all jokes, cool as a cucumber. I did admire that. The more I thought about it. The clearer my head was. He must have got that gene from his mother because it definitely wasn't passed down to me.

It made me feel guilty for being in such a state. I couldn't sort my brain out. I felt admiration and then guilt and then jealousy and then anger again. I was thinking about the bitch who handed me down my genes. The bitch who fucked off to London because she got the shits up her. Gary's Ma was sorted. Siobhán had a good job and did sports and helped out with the kindergarten in her area. That's why I was fucked in the head and Gary wasn't. He even knew about the repairman's card himself, for Jesus fuck's sake.

'We'll just get on to that cooker bloke in the morning and get a quote for the repairs. But I suppose no matter how much it is, we'll still have to get it done. We can't be having barbecues in the kitchen,' he was saying.

I went out on my own to kick the ball around. I needed to get out. I felt like every E-number I'd ever eaten was fucking tearing at my insides. For the first time in my life I actually felt

like playing Gaelic. Nobody playing football for the laugh out
on the street ever plays Gaelic, not around here anyway. It's
just not natural. It's more normal to kick a ball around on the
ground then to pick it up and toe-bog it. You'll just smash
windows then. Gaelic is something you do in school. It's like
maths or English or Irish. It's especially like Irish actually. You
do it from day one. Even the girls take it up in secondary.
They drill it into you. That's the only way the GAA get support. People wouldn't bother with it otherwise. You just can't
shake it off. It's like never forgetting that poem that goes,
'There was a boy whose name was Tom who made a high-
explosive bomb' or remembering that the angles of a triangle
add up to 180 degrees. Football stays with you because you
play it for the laugh and Gaelic stays with you because you're
made do it.

For some reason I was in the mood for picking the ball up
this time and booting it as high as I could and watching it just
fly down and smack the ground. Every time I kicked it up I
imagined it was someone's head, a different head every time.
Every second or third one I'd try to smash on the volley before
it hit the road on the way down. I also started to kick it lightly
up against the high wall and then stretch up into the air and
catch it 6½ feet from the ground. I still had a knot of tension
across my chest and this just worked it out. I felt so bad for
feeling so bad. It's hard to describe.

The ball's this sacred thing of ours. If it ever went into a
river I'd jump in after it, I swear. We've had it for so long. Gary
got it when he was small by collecting tokens for one of the
supermarkets. It was a Kevin Moran Manchester United ball.
It used to have Kevin Moran's autograph on it, although that's

been rubbed off for ages. It's been worn down into this ball of smooth whiteness, all small and hard with the air gone out, like a mint you've sucked on for ages. It's funny because Kevin Moran used to play Gaelic *and* football.

Later on I thought it might be okay to ask about getting some cash for this retreat. It felt weird asking Gary for fifteen quid. It was kind of a dodgy subject to bring up.

'I was wondering, Gary, if I could ask for a lend of something?'

'A *lend* of something?'

'Well, about fifteen quid. Well, *exactly* fifteen quid.'

'A lend! That's a good one. A lend! You *want* fifteen quid is what you're saying.'

'Yeah. Yeah. I need about fifteen pounds for something. It's this thing . . .'

'I don't give a shit what you want it for. It's *yours*, okay? It's yours. Remember what I was saying this morning?'

'What?'

'The joint account?'

'Eh . . .eh . . .'

'The joint account. For the allowance. Like I was saying this morning, it's your money as much as mine. I'm just hanging *on* to the card, rather than leaving it around in a press or whatever. So it doesn't get lost, like. But, I mean, y'know with the radio and that . . .?'

'Yeah, I think I heard you say something about that all right.'

'Well, we should try and keep that at the same level all the time. That's our expenses stock. Just take what you need from that and I'll keep on topping it back up.'

'Right. But this fifteen quid. I'll tell you what it's for,' I said.

'It's okay. I don't wanna know . . .'

'It's for the sixth-year retreat, that's all. We're going down to Powell's place in Wexford.'

'Powell's place? Oh right. The castle. I missed out on that.'

'Oh. Maybe I'll leave it.'

'No, no, Jesus, no. Go on it. I mean, I missed out 'cause I was sick, I remember. I'd paid up and all, and I got on the coach, and before we'd even got to the first traffic lights, I'd puked my ring. Ha! I remember Raffler saying that after I'd left, all the way down when they went up a hill there was this river of fucking cornflakes or whatever I'd had for breakfast that morning flowing around down the back of the bus! It was digesting the lino! But listen, I would have gone on it and all, so go on will you. Don't be thinking about the money. I mean, Jesus, *fifteen quid*! Go on.'

'All right so. Yeah. Thanks. I will. Thanks. Yeah.'

So Gary actually went over to the radio and took out the fifteen quid and put it down on the table for me. I kept on having to tell myself that he wasn't doing me a favour, that it was my money as much as his. *My money as much as his.*

'When was the last time you were out, Jer? I mean, *out* out?'

Jesus. That got me thinking. *Out* out. There was The Tankard that time, briefly. But no, *out* out. It was weeks. My birthday. That was the last time. September the thirtieth stretching into the morning of October the first.

'It's been a while, hasn't it?'

'Ah, just a couple of weeks, like. No big deal. I haven't been really feeling like it or anything. I've been having an all-right time. Really.'

'Well look. Listen. Myself and a few of the lads are going out on the town this Saturday. You should come along for the craic.'

'Nah, it's okay. I'll leave you to it. I'm doing something.'

'Bollocks! What are you doing?'

'Something.'

'Nothing. You're doing nothing. Come on out and don't be a faggot. I'm not saying it'll do you good, but you might have a laugh. You wouldn't let the side down any more anyway. There's no danger you'll get asked ID and embarrass the fuck out of us like before. Just come on! The more the merrier and all that shite.'

'Ah, I dunno. I'll leave it.'

So I left it then. I did think about it over the night though. I didn't mind Gary's mates, Paul Louden and Carl Rice and Dave McDermott and those. They were all right. It was just the old thing about hanging around with your brother's mates again; I don't know. I don't have any problems with Dave McDermott. People think I do, but I just find it a bit awkward around him; since Gary introduced me to him when he was this hardcore rocker, and he introduced me to him as this rocker brother of his, even though I wasn't, even though I couldn't grow my hair long because of the way it comes out of my head at an angle, all slanted, even though I didn't even really like the music except for one or two bands, and then Dave starts to have this conversation with me about Deathskullblahblah's new album, and I didn't have a clue, going, 'This song's not bad, that song's not bad' to everything. But I'd have maybe more in common with Dave than the other two. Carl Rice and Paul Louden are grand too, but I think Dave, strangely, on balance, is the soundest. Carl is just a bit *too* mad. You sometimes don't know which way he's going to flip. You'd be going along, and he'd see a piece of dried dog shit, and he'd say something totally hilarious about the dog shit that'd have everyone rolling around the place, but then he'd pick it up and juggle it and hold it up to his face kind of thing, and everyone'd be going, 'Jesus.' Paul though is the opposite. He's too intense for his own good. He quietens up and you wouldn't trust him. He's the kind of bloke who'd agree with everything you'd say but you wouldn't know what he'd be thinking or what he'd be saying to other people. With both Carl and Paul, there are aspects of their characters where you'd go, 'All right, they seem sound', but you could never be buddy-buddies with either of them. It's like, one would punch you in the belly and the other would rip a box-cutter down your spine. But they're an okay bunch, really.

Nah, it was just a bit sad. It was the admission. It was like, 'I've got no friends.'

Actually, I was glad I stayed in that Saturday night. There were three things I did that were worthwhile. I saw this deadly documentary on TV about these gangs, in Asia and Bangkok and places, who ran these betting syndicates that had knock-on effects for horse-racing and football in Ireland and England. It really got you thinking.

Then for the laugh I checked out all the famous people in the phone book. There were hardly any actual names. I mean, there were a couple of 'G. Byrnes' and shit, but nothing you could actually *prove* was a famous person. The weird thing was, I came across this one right out of the blue while I was

flicking through trying to look for Chris de Burgh or someone. That guy Conor Cruise O'Brien's name just popped out
at me from the page. It was his full name, and it was so clear
because it's a big odd double-barrel thing. You'd think he'd be
ex-directory because he's this Northern Ireland bloke. It's
ridiculous. People like him have their name in the book and
Gay Byrne doesn't. It's like he's saying to the IRA and the
UVF and those, 'Come on you cunts! If you want me, my
address is in the book, so come and get me!' I could imagine
him sitting there watching *Match of the Day* beneath the head
of a bear and a stuffed salmon on the wall with this big shot-
gun under his armchair, waiting, one eye on the door. I was
tempted to do a mess phone call but I didn't.

And then the last thing I did was check the calendar. And I
was lucky I did because it dawned on me that it was the three
months anniversary of Da. You have to stay in on nights like that
out of respect. I mean, I don't blame Gary for going out. I
wouldn't have realized myself if I hadn't checked. We didn't even
have one of those *month's* minds for Da, let alone whatever it is
they do after three months. I'm glad we didn't have the month's
mind. And I'm not saying that because it's like, 'Aw, Da wouldn't
have wanted it.' I mean, it wasn't Da's thing all right, all that
freaky religious shit, but *we* wouldn't have wanted it, me and
Gary. You can't dwell on these things like it's some big hang-up.
You have to move on and get on with your life. I still felt good for
having stayed in though. It was just the right thing to do.

The fifteen quid was still on the table from Gary. It had
been there for four days, pinned under the sugar bowl. The
sight of it put the thought of one phrase into my head –
monosodium glutamate; the gunk that Chinese food is soaked

in. It gives all Chinese the same flavour. They put it on everything with beef or chicken or prawns or anything meaty. It looks like diarrhoea. It's my favourite food in the world, Chinese. Whenever Da knew he was going to be off drinking after work, he'd leave some cash out for a Chinese from the Seven Samurai, these thick shits down the road who did deliveries. They weren't even Chinese. They were this bunch of chancers who'd set up this Chinese just after we'd moved in, around the time of the Chinese take-away craze when the Vietnamese boat people and those came over. 'Seven Samurai' was a *Japanese* name. I'm not one of these guys who's mad into the Japs – like, there are so many blokes who are *obsessed* with all ninjas and karate and big-eyed comics – but even I knew 'Seven Samurai' was a Japanese name. They were a godsend on nights like this though. I'd always get the same. I'd get curry chips and an omelette off the European menu, prawn crackers off the Chinese menu, and a litre bottle of Coke.

I could actually afford to splash out. After the Chinese, I'd walk it off and go over and get a few videos and some fags and a cheesecake. You have to spoil yourself every once in a while. That's what it's all about. If Gary wasn't here to enjoy it then that was his fault. I know it was money for this retreat, but fuck it. It was all going to be a waste of time anyway. I could spend this money now and have a good night and take the day off school that day instead of going on the retreat with all those dicks. I could even get more Chinese and a couple of videos on that day off, who knows? It was all nonsense. I could see it now. These crayon tracings on head-stones and having to talk to all these dicks for a whole day.

I got a few cans when I went over. It was a bit thick, because when I got back I remembered that we had a few tins of Foster's in the cupboard under the stairs. Then I started to laugh a bit to myself because it wasn't really my money, so it wasn't such a waste. I knocked the Super Ser on, put on *Die Hard 3*, had my Chinese on one side, and cracked open a few cans. This is what it's all about, I was thinking. I finished up my food and then drank my three cans over the length of the film. It was an all-right film. It wasn't as good as the first one, which was probably my third or fourth favourite film of all time, but it was better than the second one, which was way down my list but was still an okay film in its own right. I was getting a bit of a buzz going with the cans. Can't stop here, I thought. I got another couple out of the cupboard and sank them, one, two, then left it again for another while, then got another one before I went to bed, then decided to stay up and chill out a bit more, then had another one slowly over about forty minutes while I put Oasis on the stereo and made this After Eight sandwich by putting about eleven After Eights one on top of the other in a block and crunching down on them. Yeah, this is what it's all about, I was thinking. The buzz and the one moment and the one moment if you can catch it with the buzz and stay in it. That deep-heat feeling inside as you rock your head a bit to the beat and let shit just wash over you and don't care about other shit. I should do this more often, I thought. It puts shit in perspective. I sat there moving slowly backwards and forwards on the chair and listened to this music until it became a slur, until all the jingle jangle was stripped off and you could only hear the bass and I felt really, really happy, and good, and I thought, 'Things are going forward. Things are going to be all right.'

SEVEN

Some countries put a real effort into their stamps. The Czechoslovakians, and the Venezualans and Malawi – it's always the countries with nothing at all, no money, who put the care into how they look through these little bits of paper that get sent around the world. It's important, that level of attention. Sometimes it'll be the only view you get of a country. Now, when I think of Mexico, I see a yellow hummingbird. When I think of America, I only hear loud voices.

It was Da's thing, collecting stamps; from day one. He never grew out of it. In the last few years he'd be looking out for new ones from Nigeria on Uncle Phil's letters. He'd spread them on maths-copybook paper in his album. We'd stare at them for ages and he'd sometimes sniff them or rub them gently, and he'd go, 'So many countries, and that's as near as we can hope to get to most of them.' The African ones would contrast nicely with the Communist ones. You'd have all these bright colours on one page, and a predominant red with lines and angles and blokes with square jaws and flat caps hammering rivets into railway lines on another. Two different styles, but both equally as nice.

I looked down at the latest one from Nigeria and thought,

'Will I keep it?' Just for Da's sake. Hunt out the album and stick it in it. Though I suppose it was a disappointment, this one. It said 'Baobab Tree' on it and it just had a tree in the middle of a grassy plain – not the detail and the brilliance you'd expect; maybe four different colours in all. But it kind of pissed me off, the whole letter. I was looking at this stamp and then I thought, 'Hang on.' The thing about Uncle Phil's letters is that it's a given that they're for the attention of everybody in the house, and here he was addressing this one to just 'Gary Morris'. Even when Da was around, it was never just 'Bobby Morris'.

I felt shit about opening it the second I saw what was inside. It was a birthday card for Gary. I should have remembered, I thought. Only a couple of weeks from Christmas. Gary's birthday was always in that build-up period to Christmas. I really should have remembered. But then I was thinking, well, it's understandable. Then I thought again, Uncle Phil there in Nigeria and me here at home, and only Uncle Phil remembers.

I stuck the card into another envelope from the drawer and copied Uncle Phil's handwriting. Then I took the Nigerian stamp off the original envelope with lukewarm water and stuck it to the new one before it had time to dry. I handed it to Gary at breakfast, and I said 'Happy birthday' before I could stop myself.

'How nice of you to remember,' said Gary, not meaning to sound like he was taking the piss, but sounding like he was.

'I mean, it's not from me or anything. It's a happy birthday card from Uncle Phil.' *Shit*. Big fucking mouth strikes again.

Gary opened up the envelope. 'Oh, so it is. Good guess. But then, it is my birthday, and the envelope is roughly birthday-card shaped, and Uncle Phil only writes three times a year, so putting two and two together . . .'

'Look, I'll get you something later on. I forgot. I'm sorry. I don't know why.'

Gary looked at me with his mouth slightly open, then scrunched his eyebrows and twitched his head back and looked at the wall with his mouth still slightly open, like he was surprised I was apologizing.

'Ah yeah, don't worry about it, it's fine,' he goes. That kind of annoyed me too. With a normal brother, he'd have made some joke right then about me forgetting to get him something for his birthday, and I would have made some remark back, and there would have been a bit of banter. But it's like sometimes Gary underestimates my sense of humour.

'I'll get you something at the weekend when I have time.'

'Whenever, yeah. Actually, you probably won't have time this weekend. Siobhán's coming over this Saturday. She wants to take us out for the day. Treat us.'

Gary read my expression right.

'I know, I know,' he said. 'But she just feels she should be doing something for my birthday. She *is* my . . . She's . . . She mentioned you specifically. She wants you to come too. Let's face it, you're not going to bother with shopping around for a present for me,' he laughed.

Ha. Okay. Sense of humour. But he was right. I kind of knew it too in a funny way.

'Anyway,' he said, 'that's for Saturday. Tonight we —

meaning me, you, Dave, Carl, Paul and, I think, Paul's new bird – are going out.'

'Ah for fuck's sake.' I didn't mean to blurt it out like that but I couldn't hide my reaction.

'What? What's wrong? Get the fuck out of the house. Stop moping. It'll be nothing wild. Just a few scoops.'

It was getting harder and harder to avoid these situations. What was it with Gary wanting me to hang around with his mates recently? Only a while ago he would have been embarrassed about the idea. All this shit about getting out of the house. Why was it such a healthy thing? If you examine it, if you actually look into it. He was only making it difficult for me with all these offers of going out, knowing I'd only have to make up more elaborate and stupid excuses.

Carl works in this Volkswagen garage near town. He turned up at the house to meet up with Gary and then join up with the rest of them later on. He had a birthday present for Gary wrapped in goldie foil, with a bow on top and a ribbon. He comes in the door and he just stands there and takes up this discus-throwing position like that Greek statue, all this poncey posturing, and then he flings the present at Gary, and it flew perfectly through the air, going up into an arc and then hovering like a hawk for a second and then coming down slowly into Gary's hands, as if to say, as if Carl's saying, 'This discus game's a piece of piss!'

'Whoa-ho! Bit of an Al Oerter there, Carl,' says Gary.

'Who?' goes Carl. I was thinking the same myself.

'Al Oerter. Quadruple Olympic discus champion. The dogs on the street know that.'

'Right, okay. I'll take your word for it. It's not, y'know, a *touchy* subject or anything? Like, the *discus*. Not, going back to America . . .' went Carl with this sort of half-smirking, half-embarrassed look on his face.

'Oh yeah, like you're so normally sensitive about these things Ricey! Nah! Sure, I'd forgotten what a discus looks like.' Gary glanced down at the present. 'Ah, memories, mammaries!'

'Well, you haven't *looked* at it yet as such,' says Carl.

Gary ripped off the wrapping. It was a metal Volkswagen hub cap.

'Fucking hell. It flies pretty well. I mean, for a hub cap. Like, for a poxy shit like *you* throwing a hub cap.' He takes this dramatic look out the window like some toss-pot. 'Let's see if the maestro still has it.'

There'd been a real chill that day. The windows in the house had gone all steamy from the hob and the bubbling. I went scrummaging for my winter jacket at the back of the coat rack for the first time since March or something. Then the three of us went out to the middle of the road. It was pretty deadly, like the heavies, like a gang, like that thing, '*The boys are back in town, dvv-dvv da-da da, wa-a-a-ng wah!*' I hoped a couple of people would see us. The whole block down to the end of the T-junction was pretty well lit up with the street-lights. Each of us had three shadows from all the lights shining down in different directions. Gary was still in his dramatic mood. He points down, *slowly* lifting his arm and *slowly* uncurling his finger into a point, and goes, 'Right, down there', down to the house beside the Hansel and Gretel house, the Doolins I think they're called.

'It's okay Morris, we *know* you're good,' Carl was saying.

'Yeah, we know you're good,' I was saying.

Gary started to psyche himself up. He was messing, but there was a seriousness behind it. He wanted to prove to himself that he could still do it. This had been his life for years. Now here he was stuck back home doing fuck all and out of practice. He wanted to prove it to me and Carl too. Show off to Carl and rub my nose in it a bit and show who was the better person all round.

'All right Gary boy, get it together, get it together,' he was saying to himself, flipping the hub cap between his hands. He started going through the motions like he was at the Olympics, gripping the disc against his palm with his flattened fingers and swaying his arms slowly backwards and forwards around like a helicopter, getting ready for the throw.

'All right Al fucking Oer . . . Art . . . Oer . . . Arsehole, whatever,' goes Carl, 'Let's see you do it. Yo dah man!'

Gary wound himself around his spine. That's the science of it. The physics. That's what you do – you use your spine as an axle. Gary wound himself around and launched himself like a spring. That's the *theory*. That and the feet. The thing about the discus actually is the feet. Gary would always get a bit tied up it seemed to me. He launches the thing into the air but I could see it was all wrong with the feet. Too much of a shuffle and not enough of a whisk. You shouldn't hear that *chk chk chk* on the concrete. It went up pretty impressive all right. It disappeared out of sight – went right out of the light and up into the dark – but when it dropped back down again into the field of light the next lamp post down – that's a distance of around 60 feet between the two lamp posts, and it came down maybe 10 feet behind that – it was spinning like mad, not just round and round, but tossing, over and over, tossing the light off its dented surface, like a flipped coin, tossing like a fucking pancake. It came down and wobbled around really clumsily and rolled all over the place and keeled over dead.

I've seen Gary throw a real discus properly I'd say about fifteen times in my life and he's okay, I'll admit, but I was never *that* impressed. It's just throwing a frisbee basically. Granted, this was a hub cap, but it was a crap, very, very disappointing throw. It didn't deserve the 'Oh, *y-e-e-e-s-s*, suck my cock!' comment.

I had this mad idea suddenly. This hub cap flying through the air looked like one of those clay pigeons they shoot with shotguns. I was thinking, what if you could blow this thing out of the sky? How loud a noise would it make? *How fucking loud a noise would a metal hub cap, blowing up in the middle of the air, in the middle of the night, in the middle of a housing estate, make?* I don't have a gun though, naturally; I'd have to blow it up from the *inside*, sort of. I read this deadly story in an annual once about this armour-plated airship that the Germans built in World War One and they were going to drop an atomic bomb or a germ bomb or something on London. They got this pilot to fly up – this is the Brits, this is – and he lands on top of the thing and he climbs down this shaft leading to the carriage underneath and he's shooting all these Germans along the way – he's saying shit like, 'Eat lead, sausage eater' – and he jumps into this escape plane at the bottom, and just as he's breaking away from the carriage he flings one of those World War One stick grenades back into the airship and it catches fire to the hydrogen and blows it up.

Gary and Carl were going, 'Where the fuck is he off to?'

I ran back into the house and up to my room. I pulled open the bottom shelf in my chest of drawers. *Whoof* – fucking hell! The smell hit me like a green cloud – sweaty clothes I never wear any more and had never put in the wash all mixed in with the stink of stale blow I'd had stashed away since God knows. In there though I remembered was this pack of quarter sticks. I'd bought them off this guy in school years ago after he went to France; really vicious things – by quarter sticks they meant quarter sticks of *dynamite*, the real deal. We used to drop them in Sesame Street bins on the road on Hallowe'en for the echo. They'd have taken your hand off. With most bangers, the customs officers would have turned a blind eye, but not with these. With most bangers, you'd have ignored the 'Light the blue touch paper at arm's length and retire' shit, but with these it was like good advice.

I got hold of the hub cap where it landed. Gary and Carl had already lost interest. They were smoking and cracking gags down at the point where the discus was launched. Carl looked up for a second.

'What are ya up to down there, young Morris?'

I started to tape two quarter sticks to the underside of the rim with masking tape, at opposite ends to give it balance. The way I lit the fuses was deadly. I spun the hub cap around on the tip of the finger of one hand, like that plate-spinning. Then I held up my lighter to the rim with the other so that the flame lit the two wicks within a second of each other. Gary and Carl could see I was going to do a throw myself. They still weren't interested. They were chatting and laughing. Carl made some sort of gesture with his hand towards me, a sort of 'This way, boy' sign without turning his head in my direction.

I had to work quickly. The fuses on the quarter sticks gave you about a twelve-second delay, but you could never be sure. Sometimes they'd be faulty and scorch your arm and give you tinnitus for a week if you weren't careful. If you stood right up to them they'd probably rip your bowels out.

I let out a bit of a shout as I flung the hub cap into the air to let Gary and Carl know. There were sparks flying out of it like a catherine wheel that had come loose off its nail. I watched it through the air as it went. I was beckoning it to just blow up midway, going 'Come on, come on' to myself.

But it wasn't going to happen. I could see that the fuses had already extinguished themselves and it was on its way down. It hit the ground from a good height and landed with a clang banger-side down.

It was on the road about half-way between me and the lads. Gary started to peer at it. It was like he could see something that I couldn't. He sort of hunched his shoulders down and strained his eyes to look more closely, then started shifting towards the hub cap. Carl followed him. I moved up to meet them. I could see it now. The fuses had reignited.

'Jesus Christ. You fucking arsehole!' Gary was shouting, already covering his ears.

'Oh yes my son, oh *yes*,' Carl goes as it dawned on him what I was up to, always mad for a laugh.

The hub cap was fizzling and shaking like the lid of a boiling kettle. You could hear the hissing.

It died out then suddenly. Gary edged towards it again and so did I.

'What have you got there – a banger or something?' There was a bit of a smile on Gary's face. He was beginning to see the humour of it all.

'Two bangers. Two quarter sticks.'

'*Two* b . . .?' Gary stopped. He cocked his head. The fizzling started again. It spurted blue.

BANG.

Every car alarm went off in the neighbourhood. Every dog started barking. Every door knocker clunked on its clapper as every door on the road swung open.

'*Jeeeay*-zus! *Jeeeay*-zus!' Gary was hopping around cursing to himself, shaking his head and holding it with one hand.

Carl made a Y-shape with his arms, like in *Platoon*. He stood up in the middle of the road.

'Happy fucking birthday! Happy FUCKING birthday! Happy birthday from all the boys at the fucking . . . Bosnian . . . whatever . . . liberation . . . whatever . . .'

I think he'd had a few cans before he came out. The hub cap came rolling out of nowhere and hit him on the ankle. I picked it up and ran back to the house. There were two white blast-stains but not much of a buckle on either side. Gary was twisting his finger around in his earhole. It was probably fucked, the whole inside of it, but he was too giddy with Carl to be really annoyed.

'No second thoughts about coming out with us?' he goes.

'Nah, I'm okay.'

'Right. Well. The offer's there. You know where we're headed. You know where to find us if you change your mind.'

It was either a case of following them out now or not at all. Did Gary think I'd seriously follow them into town if I had changed my mind? What a joke. But it was grand. Carl was already half-way gone. A few more pints and it could get dodgy, you wouldn't know. They seemed like they were in a bit of a rush to move on.

I'd been sorting the coats out on the coat rack when Siobhán called on the Saturday morning. The coat rack had got ridiculous. You could mark out your entire life by it. It was like a cross-section through mud in a bog with all the different layers that had built up over time. All the coats fell off at one stage recently, and Gary had put them back mixed up, with baby duffel coats on top of rain gear on top of bomber jackets. We were terrible for not throwing out stuff. I've that same instinct for hoarding; I hate it all that, putting stuff in bags, but it's just that we needed some order, so that the most-used coats and jackets would be near the front.

It was kind of strange, because just as I had my hand on one of Gary's jackets, Gary's Ma rings the doorbell. I'd been expecting to hear the *clip-clop* of women's shoes as a warning so that I'd have time to get out of the way before the bell rang and allow Gary welcome in Siobhán, but the *ding-dong* just goes all of a sudden, and I was caught there with Siobhán seeing my form through the frosted glass. You'd expect that *clip-clop* with most women, but with Siobhán, she has these runners on always and she just bounds along athletically hardly touching the ground. If there's one word you'd use to describe Siobhán it'd be 'athletic'. Everything about her was streamlined and aerodynamic, even the shape of her head. There she was with her hair tight around the sides of her head and tied at the back into a bouncy pony tail.

'Jerome! Good to see you. Haven't talked to you since . . . in about . . .'

'In about . . . I don't know . . .'

'Jesus, it's about four months now. It only seems like the other week.'

She wasn't dressed formally, which was good. I couldn't have stood a stuffy dinner somewhere. She's one of these ones though who's proud of the way her figure looks at the age she is and isn't afraid to flaunt it. Like, she is only in her early forties, and she'd be well entitled still to show herself off because she hasn't aged much, but there's just something off-putting about her being Gary's Ma and wearing skin-tight leggings in front of him.

Gary appeared at the top of the stairs. He always referred to his Ma by her proper name:

'Siobhán!'

I could never get my head around that. They did only meet up around four or five times a year while he was home, but still, you'd think you'd make an effort to make the distinction between your Ma and a normal bird. In a split second then, he'd go from being really pally and familiar with her to being like a little kid. He slid down the carpeted edges of the steps in his socks and Siobhán came into the hall. Then they jumped at each other and Gary gave his Ma a kiss on the ear. She squealed as he held her and twirled her around. Siobhán made a joke about Gary needing to get back into training as she squeezed his arm, and then she gave him an envelope for his birthday – 'a little something, a contribution', she went.

In the car, Gary was filling Siobhán in on his last months at home. She nodded and responded to everything, really

seeming to take an interest. She'd take in every point and she'd
be doing these exaggerated – but at the same time sincere – 'is
that so's. You'd kind of get the impression sometimes that she
neglects him, that she couldn't give a shit, but then she does
seem to really like him, and you have to keep on telling yourself that they have this weird thing going on, and that's the best
she can manage maybe, and that's maybe the right sort of carry
on for the way both their situations have evolved. But she was
being way too casual with her driving. When she'd talk to
Gary, she'd look at him and gesticulate with every word, with
only her little finger holding the bottom of the steering wheel.

Siobhán eventually pulled up to this place with a sign that
said it served 'the Best Seafood in County Wicklow'. It was
funny, but I never saw any sea on the drive down. I wondered
how fresh their stock could be.

'I know you like seafood, Gary – I hope you do Jerome.'

'I like scampi.'

'They'll have that here, I'm sure,' said Siobhán.

'They'll have chips too Jer,' said Gary.

We settled down and ordered. I got this platter yoke in a
basket and Siobhán got a sea bass. Gary looked like he was
scrutinizing the menu really carefully, drumming his chin with
his fingers as he read down the list. Then he turned to the
waitress and said, 'Have you got sushi?' Me and Siobhán
started to laugh. The waitress shook her head.

'Try the fillet of John Dory if you want something fancy,'
said Siobhán.

'What'll that be? The side of his leg? A chunk off his waist?'
Gary looked at the menu again. 'Ah here, just give us the
platter.'

'Gary, come on, I'm treating you. Now's the time to experiment.'

'Nah, look, Jer had the right idea. I'll have the platter.'

'It's probably the safest thing on the menu,' I said. 'You could keep battered food in the fridge for ages.'

'Suit yourselves.' Siobhán bit into a breadstick, giggling and shaking her head. 'I bet the both of you have a lot in common diet-wise. I bet you're both cornflakes-in-the-morning-fry-for-lunch-and-steak-and-potatoes-at-tea kind of guys. I bet both of you value your home comforts in general. Am I right?'

'Hey, I would have had sushi if it was on offer,' said Gary.

'That's like raw fish isn't it?' I said.

'Yep. I lived off it in America.'

Gary and Siobhán were getting on better and better as the day went by. They're like a brother and sister mainly, although sometimes it can get a bit like a girlfriend and boyfriend kind of thing. Just the ebb and the flow of the banter, and the way they fall on each others shoulders, and the guffawing. Siobhán was even more careless with her driving on the return, because now she was more relaxed and in her stride with Gary. Gary would sometimes call her 'Mother', but in the way you would if you were trying to take the piss out of the English:

'Where are you taking us now, Motha?'

'Same place I always go this time on a Saturday,' said Siobhán.

'Which is?' goes Gary.

'See if you can work it out.'

'Well, we're turning off now to – I'm guessing Bray – so, well, I don't know. What do you do at three o'clock every Saturday afternoon in Bray?'

We drove up to the car park near the sea front in the town.

'Now,' goes Siobhán to Gary, 'open up the glove compartment there.'

Gary pulled down the door. 'Plastic cups. Interesting. What's this, you want a urine sample from us or something?'

Siobhán had got out of the car and taken something from the boot. She came back around holding a bottle of whiskey and a bottle of Coke. 'Jerome' – she took a cup out of the stack and gave it to me – 'myself' – she took one for herself – 'and my *baby*' – and Gary got one. 'Happy birthday son.'

'Oh. Right. Well. Cheers, Mother. Eh. Do you not want to go and sit down somewhere for a drink?' went Gary.

'Look. Are you gonna help me finish this bottle or not?'

We sat sipping at our cups, looking across the park at the one or two people walking along the promenade. Even in winter you get the odd few folks coming out to enjoy the seaside. Old people mainly, or people jogging, or people like Siobhán, out to enjoy a bit of drinking. Which was weird.

'Guys, we're not too far from the cemetery,' she goes. 'Would you like to visit your Dad's grave later on?'

It was weird because it would never have occurred to me that she'd be sort of a loner like this. But then, she was a hard one to figure out. She was sporty, and you mightn't associate the drinking with that, especially someone who'd go off drinking on their own, but then she was what some people might call a free spirit, and she was apt to do funny, flighty things, but in a good way.

'Just to pay him a visit before Christmas,' she says.

'We're okay for the moment,' said Gary. 'It'd just be a bit of hassle right now. Getting a wreath and all that.'

'It'd be no hassle. We don't have to get a wreath. Even if you wanted to, we'd get it outside the gates of the graveyard,' said Siobhán. 'Well what about you Jerome?'

'I'll go on my own some time.'

'Okay. Nah, it's only if you wanted to, guys. In your own . . . times.' She poured the last few drops of whiskey into her cup and finished them off straight. 'Right. Now that I'm nicely warmed up, I'm going have to ask the two of you to look out *that* way' – she pointed towards the sea – 'while I step outside the car for a minute.'

'What . . .?' goes Gary. Siobhán was gone to the boot again. He looked out the back window. 'She's getting a sports bag.'

'What's she doing?' I said.

'I don't know. She's getting out a swimsuit.'

I twisted around.

'Stop fucking gawking, Jesus,' says Gary.

Gary looked out again at the promenade.

'You know you want to gawk yourself,' I said.

'What the fuck are you saying you sick prick?'

'You're all like, hands-on with her.'

Gary jerked his neck and shook his head in that 'what are you on?' way. 'You sick shit,' he muttered.

There were dried-up dirt specks on the side mirror. It was hard to see properly because the sun was sinking in behind Bray and it was illuminating all the specks.

'Well what the fuck are *you* looking at?' says Gary.

'Nothing much. She's got her back turned.'

'What?'

'She's wriggling into her swimsuit.'

'Fuck's sake Jer, that's my . . . y'know, it's my *Mother* you're looking at.'

'Oh really.' I laughed. 'Hey, look what's coming.'

There was an old man with a roll-up and a Yorkshire terrier walking towards us. Gary knocked on the side window to try and warn Siobhán. Just when he was passing the car, the man diverted his eyes away from Siobhán and took this real round-about route around another car and went off in a different direction grumbling to himself. Siobhán goaded him by lifting the towel around her shoulders like a Dracula cape and going 'Not used to winter bathers, are we?', even though she was now in her swimsuit. The old bloke said something all muf-fled, wrapped the dog's lead around his wrist, made this 'up yours' gesture with his arms and spat the stub of his roll-up on the ground. Siobhán gasped at him. Me and Gary were wait-ing for her to get back at the bloke with some sharp comment. But she kind of seemed all hurt. She dropped the towel off her shoulders while still looking at the man and then spun it into a croissant shape and tucked it under her arm.

She bent down to the two of us and said, 'Anyone like to follow me?' She darted off towards the sea. Gary hesitated a moment then followed after her. He made it to the edge of the beach before Siobhán had got to the water. He jumped the three feet up on to the blue railing without breaking his stride and sprung off it and landed without scrambling. Then he seemed to stop. I could see his head and upper body over the top of the slope of pebbles on the beach. When I caught up with them, I saw Siobhán standing at the water's edge. She was turned to Gary in the middle of the beach and she was laughing. The sea was calm but it was black. She looked back at the water.

'Go for it!' shouted Gary.

Siobhán took a step behind her and ran straight in. The sea churned and thundered up under her legs. She let out this big yelp and dived forward. Then the water seemed to calm down the minute she immersed her whole self in it. She made it go in a 'V' around her. It was moving like it was making way for her, like she was its guest, or like the water had turned into liquid metal. She did this really graceful turn to her left and glided forward with hardly a splash. She submerged herself and made her legs poke vertically up from the surface like the fluke of a whale and then taper down into the water again.

A few seconds later she reappeared about 5 yards from the beach. Gary had gone up to the water's edge. He picked up what looked like a small flat stone and he flung it with a backhand on to the surface near to Siobhán. He made a messing-yell as it skipped about ten times along the water. Siobhán stood up in the shallows and started walking back. She made this mock *brrr* noise and gesture, but you knew she didn't even feel the cold.

Gary handed Siobhán her towel as she came back up the beach. She gave herself a quick drying-off and then laid it out on the shingle. She collapsed in three movements like a stunt-roll – on to her knees, a flop forward with her hands taking the fall, and a flip over on to her back. Not bad agility for someone of her age. She lay there smiling and shivering.

'Now, are you fucking *mad*? You'd be hard pressed to catch the rays even in the *summer* here, Siobhán,' said Gary.

'I'm not sunbathing, you wally. I'm keeping myself in tone. Shivering is one of the best ways.'

Siobhán's whole body was moving all manically in little tics, tense and electrical. You could see this was a regular activity for her; she was smoothed and in-shape and waxed. But if you looked closely at the tops of her thighs, the tightening skin was getting stretched around these dimples of cellulite. All the way down her legs were tiny varicose veins and pin-pricks of purple and little raised squiggles of white, like mother-of-pearl all crushed up and mixed in with custard.

I felt seedy in the throat. It was the whiskey and the Coke. I kept on tasting the flat, sugary Coke again.

It felt like a full day had passed when we got back to the house, but it was still only six o'clock. Siobhán said, 'Oh God' as she flopped into the couch, as if to say, 'Oh what a really great but exhausting day.'

'Are you going to stay for tea?' said Gary.

'I'm not hungry, but I'll stay for a while,' said Siobhán.

I wasn't hungry either. My stomach was still full from grease and whiskey and salt air.

'Guys, has anyone a couple of spare fags?' Siobhán asked. She phrased it as if she was asking both of us, but she was turned to Gary.

'Gary's just a fair weather smoker,' I said. 'His coach in America bet it out of him. Here.' I gave her one of three I had left in the pack on me.

'Keep those other two aside,' said Siobhán.

'Keep those other two aside? Ah you're not . . . You are . . .' went Gary.

Siobhán had taken out a skin from a packet of Rizlas and was kneading it out on the table. 'What's the matter?'

'Nothing. Nothing,' said Gary. 'It's just . . .'

'What? *Me*. Is that what you were going to say? Your mother smoking hash?'

Gary sniggered uncomfortably.

'It's all right then. Me and Jerome'll finish this off.' She took maybe a ten spot out of her jacket pocket. 'Isn't that right?' She winked at me. I did this forced laugh at her too. Then I threw the pack with the two fags in it down on the table, sort of automatically. But it was weird, yeah. Gary's mother.

She made out this really tidy spliff, like everything about her, all compact and sharp and streamlined. She lit it like a slapper, pursing her lips and crossing her eyes angrily to focus on it. Then she drew on it like a real classy lady, kissing her fingers and closing her eyes. When she exhaled, she made that *pff* sound that only women make, or that you imagine them making when they smoke.

When Siobhán passed it to Gary, you could see him hesitating. He'd normally not refuse, but this was just a different, strange situation. But when a spliff is being passed around the room, protocol normally just takes over. You could see the way he was thinking: you just have to be cool about it and go with it. Siobhán was enough of a stranger for him still to want to show off. I'd made up *my* mind though. I'd refuse. I'd take a stand and I'd make a point by not doing it. Gary though is that bit weaker-willed when it comes to things like this.

The two of them were already light-headed when Siobhán went to make up the second spliff. They were slunk back as far as you could get into the couch and beginning to laugh like fools. They both had their legs opened out and their knees were touching. When Gary moved position to get comfortable, Siobhán moved too. Gary's ankle was touching Siobhán's now. They were talking crap and laughing like fools. They were talking about some woman in the kindergarten that Siobhán worked in who Gary had met before. They were slagging her off about how good-looking she thought she was even though she had a lazy eye and she looked like Rodney from *Only Fools and Horses*. They were talking about how little this woman got, and then this led them on to talk more filthy talk. It wasn't straight-out filth, but it was all nudge-nudge shit and snotty laughter. For someone who'd been out swimming earlier on, Siobhán still looked like she had make-up on. She had naturally engorged lips and sharp corners on her eyes. She was very unmotherly. She was hard, not soft. She was like a slab of muscle. I watched with disgust and wonder the rally of words between them. It got worse and worse the more drags on the spliff each of them took. When I looked down at their legs again, the insides of their ankles were touching.

Siobhán offered me the the end of the spliff.

'I don't want it. I didn't want any of the last one. I don't want any of this one,' I said.

She gave a 'fair-enough' raise of her eyebrows and drew back on the end of the spliff until the embers almost burned white.

'And I don't care if you think I'm a prude for not taking it,' I said.

The two of them were flaked out on the couch, floppy as the cushions.

'I probably seem like a prude to both of you, though. I

mean, I'm just being normal, but the way the two of you are carrying on . . .'

Siobhán turned to Gary as if she was slowly waking out of a deep sleep. When she opened her mouth she was croaky. 'Could you call me a taxi Gary? I won't be driving home tonight,' she said.

Gary dragged himself up.

'The way you're *carrying on* . . .' I said.

'What do you mean, Jerome?' said Siobhán.

'The way you're talking, the two of you!'

'We're only having . . . a laugh. Gary . . . should feel comfortable enough with me at this stage to be able to talk . . . about anything. I feel comfortable enough with him to be able to talk about anything. That's the thing about me. People can talk to me about anything.'

'No! You're just talking shite! It's not like he's reached the stage where he can talk to you about anything as a Mother. As a kid, like . . . as a son might do to his mother. You're talking like some slapper and some dickhead! *You're his fucking mother! You're his Ma! You're his Ma!*

'You're over-reacting a bit Jerome. We're not saying anything particularly bad.'

I went out into the hall. I went to shout at Gary but he was on the phone. I didn't want him to be interrupted calling the taxi because I wanted Siobhán out of the house. I went back into the TV room.

'*You're a fucking slapper! Look at you! Lying there!*

Siobhán had produced this small brass bong from somewhere. She was taking puffs from it and was slumped back more casual than before. Her eyelids were half-way down her eyes but she was looking up at me like she was calm and content. I felt as if I'd screamed part of my brain out. It felt like there was a chunk gone from the core of my head somewhere. This terrible headache came over me and the smoke in the room made me feel dizzy. I fell down on my knees and rested my forehead on the little table in front of the couch.

'Are you okay?' I wasn't sure whether Siobhán was slurring her words or whether the distortion was coming from inside my head.

'I think I might be sick,' I said. 'I'm going to go to the toilet.'

I got up to go. When I reached the toilet, I turned on the light. It was a bare bulb with too strong a wattage hanging from this scrawny wire. There was no shade around it. It blasted the room with cold light. I turned around and went back past Gary into the TV room.

'Siobhán. Could you come with me?' I said to her.

With only the normal hesitation you'd expect from someone who's stoned she got up and followed me back. I heard her pat the walls behind me as she steadied herself.

I went in and knelt over the bowl.

'Siobhán. Could you hold my head while I get sick?'

She put her hand to my forehead. The room was freezing. The radiator was broken and the light put the shivers in you. But Siobhán's hand felt warm. Her hair was down now. I hadn't noticed before, but when I saw her reflection behind mine in the water in the bowl, her head was blocking off the light from the bulb, and strands of her hair were silhouetted behind my head.

'It's okay now Siobhán. I don't feel sick any more. I think the sickness has passed.'

She let go and I stood up. Her eyes were fully open now; she tilted her head slightly as she looked into mine. She held me firmly by the shoulders and asked me was I okay. Then she moved her hands around my back and put her chin on my shoulder and hugged me tightly.

'When you said people can talk to you about anything Siobhán, does that mean I can talk to you about anything?' I said.

'Yes.'

'Can I ask you anything? Something?'

'Yeah.'

'Well, you were going out with my Da, before I was born, right, and that's when you had Gary. But you sort of kept in touch and, like, did you know much about who my Da was going out with after I was born?'

'Yeah.'

'And, well . . .'

'Yeah.'

'Siobhán, can you think straight?'

'Yeah.'

'Let's go back inside.'

'Your mother was like a beautiful swan.'

'Siobhán, do you mean that?'

She started laughing. 'I don't know. Come here. Give us another hug.'

We sat down, the three of us, on the couch, not saying anything, until the doorbell rang.

When I opened the door there was this guy there with a bright red baseball cap and a pizza box. He held out the box to me and he went, 'That'll be nine sixty please.'

I left the guy at the door and went back to Gary.

'Gary, do you know anything about a pizza?' I said.

'This *is* the right address?' the guy shouted back. He read out the address written on the box.

'Yeah, yeah. It's the right address. Sorry about that,' Gary shouted back at the guy.

'Sorry about what?' the guy said.

Gary turned to me and Siobhán. 'Any of you want some of this pizza now that it's here?'

'I'm not hungry,' said Siobhán.

'Neither am I,' I said.

'Did you order me a taxi?' said Siobhán.

'Ah, sorry. I meant to,' said Gary. 'Must have been the sub-conscious munchies coming through.'

'I'd like to take a rummage 'round *your* fuckin' subcon-science,' the pizza man shouted back in, messing. 'You ordered pepperoni, ham, chicken, onions, sweetcorn, dough balls and pine nuts.'

'Ah Gary now, come on, ring me up a taxi,' said Siobhán. Her words were urgent but she didn't say them in an urgent way.

'Where are you headed?' the pizza man suddenly said to Siobhán. I just looked at the guy, going 'What the fuck?' to myself.

'Back in towards town,' said Siobhán.

'Well I'll tell you what,' said the pizza man. 'This is the last delivery on my shift. Somebody pay for this pizza, then I'll bring you back into town.'

Siobhán didn't even question the pizza man. She already had her coat on her shoulders. She gave Gary a half-nelson

sort of hug and me a kiss on the cheek and walked out to the
guy's car. She shouted back something about collecting her car
the next evening. She left it for the guy to close the door. He
nodded at me as he did so. I had this image flash into my
mind after the car had taken off of Siobhán's body being
stabbed and smashed up in the Dublin mountains somewhere.

It was a stupid thing to take a lift off someone you didn't
even know. I'd wanted to say something, but I automatically
felt that it was Gary's place to object. Siobhán needed a decision made for her. In the absence of someone speaking up, she
was just going to go with whatever option was presented to
her. But there was no point in letting fly at Gary. It was comical. You could have pressed your little finger on his nose and
he would have fallen over. It was sad. You look up to your big
brother when you're young. It was pathetic. I looked at him
flop around the place and I just thought, 'pathetic'. He was a
pathetic figure tonight. He was getting sick in the toilet.

EIGHT

I wouldn't say Christmas just came and went, but pretty much. We were never ones for the frosty spray on the window or the outdoor lights anyway. We don't even have a tree in our front garden to put lights *on*. We don't even really have a front garden. You wouldn't call it a garden as such. There's not much grass and no flowers or gnomes or sea-shells in it. It's mainly tarmac although that's hard to tell from the grass because of all the moss on it these days.

I'm all for the idea. You moan about it and buying people presents and shit, but when it comes around you really appreciate the break and the deadly films. You really start to dread 7 January and you get taken over by this total feeling of sadness when it comes and you have to go back to school. That's the thing about Christmas actually. Sweets and Christmas are the two things in life guaranteed to make you sad. Looking at jars of sweets stacked up in a shop window and the whole Christmas thing – the lights, the tinsel, the old boxes; all that.

I mean, nothing really happens, but that's okay. The buying presents is okay too. There was never really much of a problem in our family. I'd always have a bit of money set aside from working over the summer down at the garden centre and I'd only have to get two presents. Me or Gary never even had to bother with Uncle Phil. Da used to just buy something for him and pass it off as a present from us. There was this kind of unofficial promise from me and Gary that we'd pay the money off to Da later on. Like, he'd go out and buy the present on the sly sort of thing and come Christmas Eve he'd go, 'So what did you get your Uncle Phil then?' and we'd be going, 'Shit' and pretend to look all embarrassed and then he'd go, 'Ah, you're gas, the two of you! Come up with the quids no later than New Year's Eve', knowing damn full well that we wouldn't bother. But then by February or whatever we'd forgotten we even *had* an Uncle Phil, so it was the same old story the next Christmas. Uncle Phil himself was always quite decent because we were practically his only family, and even now that he's married, him and this African bird are probably too old to have kids. After he went to live in Nigeria, he was only able to come back home at really awkward times because of whatever work they were getting him to do, and never at Christmas, because it's all different over there with Christmas and their beliefs. There was always a cheque in the post though. Last Christmas he was extra generous because of the whole Da situation. We got a thousand quid, which went straight into the account. And of course, being in Nigeria and not having Da to buy a present for us to give him – I think Uncle Phil was in on the scam – we weren't expected to send *him* over one. So Christmas was that little bit easier this year. There was just Gary to buy for, and I got him this supply of powdered liver for his discus, which is what I've been getting him every year for the past few years.

And you've the drink as well; a big two-week piss-up; an excuse to get completely shit-faced. Which is fine, I've no problems with that. It had become part of my Christmas tradition too, like the toys and the chocolate when I was younger. But I'd usually do my own thing. The previous Christmas it was Cynthia. The few before that me and Ultan Collins used to go knacker-drinking down at the jungle.

It was The Tankard this Christmas Eve. I allowed myself to be manipulated. Gary has ways of talking me into anything when my defences are down. I hadn't any excuse lined up. It was getting wearying with these excuses. It was me and Gary and Gary's old mates all off down to The Tankard.

But I decided I'd just throw myself into it and enjoy it. You never know, I was thinking. Let bygones be bygones. It was only once a year. You have to say, 'Fuck it, it's Christmas' at times like this. Everyone does.

I decided I'd throw myself into it with the aid of a few cans beforehand. I checked the cupboard under the stairs but there were no cans left. I'd have to go to the off-licence. When I went down and saw the whiskey I changed my mind. I'd get some whiskey. It was Christmas. Whiskey warms your spirit. I bought a small bottle of Paddy and then went on my way home past the jungle. I stopped to look in. There was a huge dual-carriageway lamp post towering overhead and the light was filtering down and you could see in amongst the shrubs. It looked just like old times. 'Ah here,' I said, 'for old times' sake.' I made my way in along a little path that had been beaten out by some other kids. The ground was covered in muck and leaves and it was a bit slippy. Then I got into my little spot. The same old spot. This little hollow right in the centre. The way the leafless branches arced up into a dome around you, it was like a den. It was all immaturity back then, really, the way you were breaking out on your own by going off and drinking, but at the same time you needed the comfort of a den, like a kid. The first Christmas I went out was a bit of a joke. It was just me and Ultan Collins and we'd got ourselves a couple of cans of some six-for-four-quid shite and we came down here, just the two of us, trying to look all hard and convincing ourselves we were having a laugh. Us and all these other lads in the area; little gangs, freezing our bollockses off in the shrubs.

I took a few good swigs from the bottle of whiskey and looked up around me. I wondered how many plastic bags those branches had been through since I used to come here. Tatty bags caught up in the air surging down the dual-carriageway and then getting trapped in the shrubs and rattling in the wind. They were cold nights always, I remembered. The snot would be dripping down. It was gas. The only thing warm was the beer. That was from my two hands clasping the can, rubbing it and sort of caressing it, not knowing really what to say. The metal would split at the corners of the folds of the can. I'd sometimes scratch and cut my palms and the beer would trickle out. But I didn't mind that too much. It would go quicker. You could fake it; fake knocking it back. The beer used to make me sick back then. Drink definitely is an acquired taste.

Ultan. This was of course before the Collinses moved out to Castleknock or somewhere and I never heard from the fucker again.

I threw the empty bottle down for the rats with all the rest of the rubbish and continued on my way back home. A Christmas night in The Tankard, I was thinking. The usual crowd multiplied to the power of a hundred.

*

Everyone was buying their rounds except me. I was excused. It was shitty. I didn't want that and I didn't ask for it. After it had come full circle, through Gary, through Carl, through Paul Louden, through Dave and then to me, I stood up with my hand in my pocket, but the lads just protested. I kept on offering but they kept protesting. I'd get up with my hand in my front pocket and sit down with my hands in my back pockets. I gave in easily but felt bad for it.

I would have objected though to getting Paul's new bird Esther a drink because she wasn't buying any rounds for anyone. All the lads were sucking up to her because she was all-right looking, as if there might have been a chance of a ride or something. I don't know. They were going along with Paul's insistence. He wouldn't have his bird buying rounds and that was that, not Paul's bird, oh no no no. But the other lads were buying her a drink on *their* rounds.

Paul was the most eager of the lot. *Obviously*, like. It was obvious that they'd either ridden earlier in the day or that they'd planned to do it that night. You could see it, the eager-ness. I mean, it was obvious to have it whittled down to those two options but it was still hard to tell if it was one or the other. If The Tankard hadn't been so heavy with smoke I'd have been able to tell. The tell-tale smells. You can tell the smell of dried-up sex on the inside of thighs and on bellies easily. The friction and the liquid makes a froth. It hangs in the air no matter how hard you scrub. There's no need to make an effort to clean up too much and impress each other then because the deed is done. You're on the way down. What you'd hope to build up to at the end of the day is over before the night is done; it's nature. If I'd been choking with the toiletries, the Bics and the Hugo Bosses, if they'd been all dollied up, then it would have been option B. Actually, it probably was option B. They were all glances and winks and not completely comfortable with each other. It was a bit sick, some of the gestures and things they were saying. I'm not saying I'm an expert on these things, but they were even making the lads uneasy by a certain stage.

She didn't look at me all night, this Esther. It was good in a way me getting out of buying rounds because the thought of buying a drink for that tart would have gnawed at me all night. I wouldn't have been able to enjoy the evening. I would have added up all the cash spent on her in my head and thought of all the videos or what tape or how many more drinks for myself I could have bought. I didn't see why I couldn't buy drinks for the lads though.

'Are you gonna stare at that drink all night, young Morris?'

I wasn't keeping up with the lads. There was a steady queue of pints forming in front of me. I'd got through half of one – Gary's round – and there was another full one behind that which I think either Paul or Dave got. Everyone else had empty frosted glasses in front of them.

'Cmoncmoncmoncmoncmoncmoncmon!' Carl was rapping the table with his knuckles as he got up. 'C'mon. My round. Keep up with big brother.'

Fuck off, fucking cunt.

'Same again everyone?'

'Same again,' said Gary and Paul, together, nodding.

'Make mine black and white again,' said Dave.

Paul's bird muffled something in Paul's ear and both of them giggled and then she turned and said herself, 'I think I'll have a Hooch this time.' I thought I heard Dave muffle 'spreaders' in Gary's ear. Carl turned to me.

'Havin' the same again Je . . .? . . . Jaysus! You're catching up!'

I'd knocked back the rest of the first pint and was most of the way down through the second one in about twenty seconds. Less, even.

'It's all right Jer,' Gary starts up.

'It's all right *what*?' I asked.

'It's all right like, you don't have to . . .'

'I don't have to *what*?'

'It's all right,' he said. He went back to what they were all talking about before. 'So. Anyway. You can say "trouser", but you can't say "*scissor*".'

'But that's bollocks,' goes Dave. 'I mean, you're no more gonna buy half a pair of trousers than you are half a fucking scissors. What would you do, like? Walk around with one leg of a pair of pants like some – I dunno – Julian Clary or something?!'

'It could be what a one-legged man would ask for. He'd go into a shop and say "I'd like to buy a *trouser* please",' said Esther, thinking she was funny.

'No, I'm telling you, you do say that saying, "trouser". It exists definitely,' said Gary. He finished off his pint. 'Who gives *two hoots* anyway? *Two hoots*. Who started this?'

I was making little piles with ripped up beer mats. They were like those things, those caveman things, those cairns. You do use that word 'trouser' when you're saying – or when a guy in a shop says – 'This is a fine make of trouser, sir.' I felt something stick in my throat and I had to cough a bit. I thought a bit of beer mat had dropped into my drink.

'So poor old Father Sleazy then,' says Paul all of a sudden.

'Yeah. S'pose,' said Dave.

I wondered what they were on about. I looked at Gary and was glad to see that he looked confused too so that he could ask them.

'What's wrong with him?' he asked.

'Ah, did you not hear?' says Paul. 'It's his liver. He's gone into hospital. His liver has completely shut down.'

'Jesus. Didn't hear that now,' said Gary. 'He had it coming, really though, didn't he? Loved his drink.'

'He's gone into a coma,' went Dave.

Carl came back with the drinks.

'Fair play the man! How'dya manage that?!' said Dave. 'One, two, three, four, *five* drinks!'

'Well, y'know what they say about people with big hands,' said Carl.

'No actually, I don't,' went Paul. '*Small* knob?'

'Ah . . . yeah . . . right . . . okay . . . ah fuck it. I'm pissed, lads. I love you loverboy. Anyway, how did you think I managed to carry all these . . . drinks . . . with . . . without . . . not having a big cock . . . or, I mean, that is to say . . . having a big cock? To balance them on. Or is that *small* cock? Let's see . . . big hands . . . big feet . . .' Carl looked over at Esther. 'Sorry ladies, to be such a . . . *scum*. I'm a real gent actually. Amn't I lads? Actually? Amn't I actually?'

Everybody seemed to be in stitches. 'Take a seat man,' said Dave, sitting him down. He put his arm around Carl's shoulders and shook him like he was showing him off to the others. 'I love this guy! I *love* this guy!'

'And,' Carl went on. He put his hands up in the air like he

was calling for a bit of hush. 'And that's not all. Did anyone of you young ladies and gents notice anything out of the ordinary as I was walking down here tonight? Walking down. Here. To the table. With the drinks. Here. Tonight? Apart from the cock.'

I looked around and everyone was still cracking up.

'Well I'll tell you. Master McDermott almost had it there a while ago with his one, two, three, four, five.'

Still laughing. I tried to laugh.

'*Six*! You see! Six! Where's number six? Where'd number six go? Where'd my drink go? Well I'll tell you. I'll show yiz all.'

Carl was still wearing his black puffer jacket, his E-dealer's jacket. He opened one half of it.

'Ta-da!'

His drink was sticking out of the inside pocket. It looked like an empty glass from where we all were because the level of the drink had gone down below, or was maybe just about in line with, the slit of his pocket. There was drink all down the inside of the jacket.

'Ah that's great Ricey! That's a great trick. A round of applause is in order. A round of applause for the man!' says Dave half-standing up clapping.

'Ah that's fierce impressive all right,' chips in Paul.

I drank my pint down in nearly one go again.

'There's only one thing,' says Paul again, and he nudges his bird. 'You got that trick off someone else. Who is it who does that trick?' He clicked his fingers. 'Who is it again? Gary, who's yer man who does that trick with the pint?'

'I dunno Paul. That's the first time I've seen it and I think it's fierce impressive too,' went Gary. 'Oh no. Hang on.

You're right, yeah. Eh. No. Gone. I've forgotten again. Some singer.'

'Who is it? Nobody. It's nobody else's. It's my trick. Show me the fucker and I'll sue him,' said Carl. He leans into my ear, giggling and dribbling, and whispers: 'I'll sue the fucker. Won't I Jerome? It's my trick. I'll sue him.'

I'd been holding myself in. I'd only had two trips to the bogs all night. It was a combination of not being able to get away and wanting to hang around for more info on Father Vesey. I held it all the way through. I kept thinking of Da's catheter that led to this container for draining the piss into after the operation. The nurse called it his handbag for a joke. It felt like there was this hacky sack weighing down at the bottom of my guts or somewhere.

I banged the bog door with my hand and almost shattered the wavy glass. I caught a look of myself in the mirror.

I wasn't all that bad looking, I thought to myself. I wasn't all that bad. Birds could go for that.

'Ah man,' I kept saying. 'Ah man.'

This bloke comes up behind me and puts his hand on my collar bone.

'Y'all right mate?'

'Ah man.'

I thought my forehead would steam up the tiles, but actually it was the other way around. The tiles transferred their temperature to my head. They were freezing. I was getting an ice-cream headache from it but I didn't lift my head. I needed to steady myself over the urinal.

I wanted to chew on one of the blue tablets. They smelled so good. My mickey was half hard as I swilled around on them. I wasn't sure for a second if it was on the way up or on the way down. I had to struggle to find an angle for it for a second. It needed a push downwards and I had to bend my legs a bit. Then it started to get easier and I knew it was on the way down. I was left with this heavy piece of meat in my hands. For the first time ever I was aware of the weight of it. I slapped it with my palm to get the last few drops out. It made a noise like *pants*. I slapped it again. *Pants*. Then I slapped it again. *Pants*. *Pants. Pants.* I hit it then with the back of my hand. It was a different sound this time. More like *thrap*. *Pants* and *thrap*.

Next I turned for the cubicle.

'Straddle the latrine,' I said to myself.

'What?' some bloke goes.

'Ahm-a gonna be straddlin' the latrine.'

I went in and I shat all this shit out my hole.

They had a thick red rope partitioning off the stairs. The stairs were to the right of the bogs as you came out. The gold hooks were latched on to two brass hoops fixed at that height that made it awkward to either step over or stoop under. I just undid it instead. The stairs up was this claustrophobic tunnel. Everything smelled of old smoke. Everything was red and gold but it was just tack. The red carpet was hemmed in at the joins in the steps by gold bars going across. I trailed my hand along the wall as I went up. More red on the walls. More *wine* actually. Furry velvet wallpaper. More tack. I took off some painting half-way up. Some old photo of the area. I just dropped it at the top. It whooshed like a hovercraft for a second on a cushion of air and then settled on the floor.

The lights were off in the restaurant but the curtains were

open. Just enough sick yellow light was streaming in from the street to be able to see. It was like that rhyme, ''Twas the night before Christmas and all through the house, not a creature was stirring, not even a mouse.' Everything was laid out for Christmas dinner for the day after. Bluey delicate glasses and coke glasses were upturned on tables for families, fourteen circular tables going around this central long one. Each place mat had a set of cutlery wrapped in tissue and a cracker at the top. The nicest touch was bowls of sugar with pink and white cubes in them. The white ones seemed to glint in what little light there was. I hadn't seen pink ones since we got our tetanus shots in low babies.

There was an upstairs tree in the corner. It was plugged out. It was just sitting there. I thought, 'Go on.' I crept along the floor under the frosty branches all slithery. There were presents, but they flitted away really easily; they were just empty cardboard boxes covered in crepe paper. The socket board on the ground at the back was holding this wedge of wires and cracked plastic and masking tape together. I lay flat down stretching for the main socket in the wall. My ear was pressed on the carpet. There were no needles. I could hear the din below the floor.

I thumped in the main plug. *Phut. Phut.* About seven bulbs went bang out above my head. Then another couple. *Ping. Phut.* All the others came on brilliantly. I held my breath for a second. Then they suddenly went out again. Then on again. Old flashing lights. Great stuff. Blinkers, we used to call them. I turned on my back to look up through the branches. It was a great show. A big box of sweet wrappers. It was like a trip.

Oranges, purples, blues, reds. Shadows. Shapes. On and off, on and off. Actually, no. Nothing was in sync actually. It was more on, on, off, on, off, off, off, on, on, on, on. Different sets set up to different times. Different levels of brightness and dimness depending. I kept thinking of the coconut ones in Roses. Sick. The thought. The colours and the flashing and the slints of light through the fibres were making me queasy. The heat. The smell of the socket board. There were thuds and booms downstairs. Breathe easy man, I was saying. Control. Control. It was making me queasy and sweaty. I could feel my pulse in my throat.

'Ah man. Ah man.'

Shit.

No air was coming in. There was a tightness.

All this pounding. I jumped up. My head went through the lower branches. The tree just lifted and there was a big tangle. It was secured only in a light sort of bakelite base. It lifted and flew and the socket board jarred it in the air and I was stuck in the branches. I had to fight it off. The tree came off but there were hot ancient wires around my arms and bits of my chest. There were spiky bulb covers pressed into my shoulder blades and the pits at the bottom of my neck. *No!* Shit. I thought I was electrocuted for a second. I waited for the shock. My teeth ground. Shit. I thought about my fillings. Shit. And my leather soles. Shit. Shit.

I waited. I thought: *Please. Phew. Gone. Please. Be gone. Passed. Passed I think. Danger passed.* Gone.

I held my breath again and then slowly unravelled the lights. My knees felt like only the cartilage was left in them. I had to sit down in the seat for a while. I gave it a moment.

I got up again then. I felt great. The pumping in my ears died down after a second.

That was another nice touch, the spoons. A table for the whole area was set up at the side for all pick 'n' mixing cutlery. They were good spoons. Set aside only for Christmas. They jangled in the tray. I picked up a big bunch of them and spread them out in my hand like a deck of cards. I grabbed as many as I could fit. I could fit so many in each hand. I liked the feel and the weight and the temperature of them. It felt like there were twenty in each hand. There was a larger soup spoon which I patted my palm with. I liked the power of that and the sound. It was old pewter or cheap metal done with electrolysis or something. The leaf was peeling off and it was warmer than the rest. I sat up on the table, crossed my legs and used it to test my knee jerk. The MOT, as they say across the water, as Da used to say about England. Everything was okay. Proper working order. Then I stuffed the spoons in my pockets and headed back down.

Carl was coming out of the bogs.

'The man! How've . . . Where's you've . . . been? What's that bulge in your pockets? No. Don't actually. Don't tell me you're pleased to see me. I don't wanna know.'

'Spoons. I've got spoons.'

'Spoons?! You're gas. I love you. You're more gas than your brother. I love you more than life itself. Cmonletsgetsome drinks.'

We moved towards the bar like wounded soldiers, the pair of us.

'Jaysus. They make a fair noise, don't they, your spoons? Some jangle.'

We nuzzled in between a couple of stools at the bar.

'Airport security. Coming through. Coming through. Beep,

beep. Oooh, what's this? Spoons, you say? *Spooooonz?*

Carl put in his orders. Lou Byrne was looking fairly pissed off. 'I think you've probably had enough for tonight now, don't you think? Just settle down a bit.'

'Ah come on. Just two black and tans, Lou. Two black and tans. Hey, he's got spoons.'

'Don't mind that dick, Carl,' I went. 'Here, try this other bloke.'

Carl asked the other barman. 'Two black and tans.'

'And I'll have one as well.'

'No, I've already ordered for you, you tit. It's all on me. I told you. I love you.'

'Then I'll have two of those . . . *sambucas* as well.'

Bang, bang, bang, bang. All the drinks were lined up on the counter.

'Here, what do you call these ones again?' I asked.

'Black and tans. And red all over. Here, what's black and white and red all over? The Black and White Menstrual Show.'

'Well look.' I poured the sambucas into the pints and there was a bit of a spillage. 'Blackjack and tans.'

'Blackjack and tans. Fair enough. I won't argue with that. Watch. Down in one.'

'Down in one.'

Carl had mastered the art. I spluttered a bit. Glug. Glug. Mostly it went down like sardines though, bones and all.

'Hey, let's get back to the lads. I mean . . . don't get me wrong. We don't *need* them, like; we've got it all right here. Just the two of us. You and me. But they've been wondering where you've been. Your big brother. Coochy coochy coo. C'mon.'

'Here, what do you think of Louden's bird?'

'Bit snotty. Still though . . .'

'Hm.'

'C'mon.'

A group of people with sort of tinsel crowns had joined the table. It was all so gay, like, 'Look at us.' They'd hoisted over a load of stools and now there was this big congregation. I figured they were a bunch of old people from Gary and Carl and Paul's year, from when they were at school. A couple of birds I did recognize, from way ahead in school who'd left ages ago.

'Wa-hey. The prodigal sons have returned,' went Dave.

'Santy and his little helper,' goes Gary.

Some bird had taken my stool. She was sitting on my jacket. I sat down on the edge and she gave me a look but then didn't seem to mind.

'Hi.' She smiled. 'What's your name?'

'Blackjack.'

'Blackjack?'

'Hey, what's black and white and – this is a joke by the way – what's black and white and red?'

'Tell me.'

'Black and white menstruation. Heh. Good one. Isnit?'

Another snotty cow.

There were bits of drinks lying all over the place. I took up some half-empty glass and took a swig. This alcopop was just *there* in front of me. Then I took some other pint.

'Fuck's sake. What's goin' *on* here?!' some fuckhead mouths off.

Gary looks up. 'Jer. Come on. I'll buy you another drink if you want.'

'Go and sit on your fucking dick.' I took another mouthful of something.

'Who the fuck is this?' – the same fuckhead – 'He's nickin' my *fuckin'* pint!'

'Ah, no one Ferg. He's just my brother. Come on Jer. Leave it. I'll get you another.'

'I *said*, fuck you.'

Good old Carl. He's cracking his shites. 'Show them your spoons Jer.'

'Oh yeah. My spoons. I'll get me spoons.'

I got my spoons. I put my hands in my pocket and got out the spoons. 'Look at my spoons!' Two handfuls of them. Jangly and bunched together. I shook them about. 'Look at my spoons!'

The bird on the stool began to wiggle. 'Who is this fucking looper?!'

'Look at my spoons!'

'Jer,' Gary starts up.

'Look at my *spoooonz*!'

'Jer. Put them away.'

'Fuck you. Look at my beautiful spoons. Who will buy my beautiful spoons? *Who will buy my beau-ti-ful spoo-oons?*'

I was shaking them across the table, up to people's faces. Carl was rolling around. Dave was smiling. Paul and his bird were staring. Gary was staring. Everybody was staring. Everyone was staring at me.

'Jesus . . . I think . . . *uuugh* . . . no . . . doesn't . . . matter. No,' Carl went. Then he stopped laughing. He seemed to run out of steam. Dave stopped smirking then. No one was talking.

'Look at my fucking spoons!'

'Jer. Please. Cop on.'

The closing-time bell starts to ring. It deadened then. Somebody put a hand over it. It was Sid. He killed it like something else caught his attention. He comes over.

'Right. Where'd you get them?'

He was towering over me. I couldn't fight it when he was looking down at me over his bags, staring down. He was drilling me into the ground. He had the psychological advantage just for that second. I stood up to look him in the eyes. People thought I was going to start on him. Gary hops up and hugs me down into the seat again. 'It's all right Sid, we're going now. We'll leave these here. He's only messing.'

This Ferg speaks up for the new group. 'Listen Gary, we're gonna split anyway. You're not coming to Marion's do, no?'

'Nah, it's all right Ferg. Myself and the lads are gonna head home. Have a good one anyhow. Canno. Kay. Paula. Fee. Mick.'

'Ladth and ladieth! Closing time!' Sid was waving around the lounge.

'Ta. Happy Christmas,' goes Ferg to Gary.

The tinsel gang went off. That bird gave me a filthy look. Gary was standing. Carl had his head back on the seat and Dave had his head in his hands on his knees. Paul looked shattered. Paul's bird had her coat on her shoulders.

'. . . Come on. The retht of you. And take thith pup with you. There better not be any damage up there.'

'Ah man.'

'Come on! Shift.'

My jacket was warm from sitting on it. I felt something

press in the inside pocket. *The last quarter stick*. I forgot. I'd left the pack in the jacket of my winter coat from that time with Carl and Gary. We all lumbered away. Sid squeezed my arm before the door. He had it like a vice.

'I'm theriouth about that damage by the way. If there'th anything . . .'

'Thhhhhhhh . . .'

'Hey. Now lithten now. What age are you? I don't know if you should be *out*, you pup. I'm not sure you should even be out. Were you up above? *Any* damage, and I'm telling you . . . *any* damage . . . Your folkth will hear about thith, believe me.'

I felt the bulge through my breast pocket in my shirt. The hard cylinder there. Mm. It felt so powerful, like all this stuff was packed into it.

'Doeth anyone know thith guy'th folkth? Ith he local?'

We moved into the porch, between the two sets of glass doors. There was noise and then a muffle as the doors behind me opened and then shut closed with the spring and people began to fill up in the space.

This old man goes by me on his way out. He ruffles my hair.

That other group were out in the car park. They were hanging around still. That snotty bird spots me again. She was sort of shaking her head. She was looking at me and squinting. Then she nudges someone and points over. My scalp was all tingly from that old man. So there's these two birds now pointing and sniping some shit about me.

'Yeah, fuck it,' I was thinking. *The banger. Fuck it. Let's do it.*

I jammed it in my mouth. I had an inch of it in and bit

down on the paper. I just rammed it in. It smelled of paper caps. I could see in the mirror in the porch the silver sparkles on my lips. I bit in hard. I *chk-chk*-ed on my lighter. I held it up to the fuse but the flint was going. Another fucking faulty lighter from Brian Waters' brother's shop. I kept *chk-chk*-ing. There were only flashes and sparks that disappeared after each *chk*. I pushed the banger in further until I was gagging. I *chk-chk*-ed again.

'Hey! Jesus! Hey! Jer! No! Fuck!'

Gary smacked the lighter away, then my face, then the end of the banger. It sent my head vibrating. I pressed my hand on the mirror to get my balance. I looked down and the banger dropped to the marble. Ha. This was funny.

'You're fucking mad. What were you doing?! What the *fuck* were you thinking?!'

The doors behind banged open.

'Come on. Get going there. Thtop blocking the way.'

Gary turns to talk with Sid again. Dave had his arse pressed up leaning against the mirror. He was bending forward holding his knees. He was looking up at the commotion. There was a fag burning in his fingers. There was a fag burning in his fingers. There was a fag burning in his fingers.

Sssssssssss. Oh yes.

'Right. Thith ith it. *You!* You're barred! You're never thetting foot in thith plathe again!'

'Thhhhhhhh . . .'

Sssssssssss.

'What . . .what'th that?'

'Thhhhhhhh . . .'

Sssssssssss.

'What *ith* that?'

'Thhhhhhhh. Thtrawberrieth. Thparrowth. Theckth.'

Sssssssssss.

'Jer, for fuck's sake, no!'

Gary could see it was too late. He tried to flick the banger out of my hand again but it just flopped and rolled on the porch floor. Half the people ran back through the behind doors into the lounge again and some of the people legged it into the car park. I went into the car park. This girl and a bloke got all confused and stayed in the porch. The bloke wrapped himself around the girl's head and the bloke covered his own ears.

The doors dampened the bang down to a thud. This initial burst but no echo. It was like when you say 'fuck' by fizzling the 'f' and braking hard on the 'ck' sound, the way it just explodes off your lips, like Americans: '*Fuck you, muthafucka!*' The security glass went *crack!* but the metal mesh held it together. The space in the porch was all milky with smoke.

And after the thud then, this whimper. A couple of seconds of silence and then the only sound was the girl in the porch crying. One or two cars going by had stopped to look, so there was no noise, just this girl crying. The gang in the car park were all 'What the fuck?' The girl comes out of the doors with the bloke, who was holding one of his ears. She wasn't in hysterics or anything, just whimpering gently on his shoulder. The bloke was stroking her hair with his other hand. Then the gang gets all stroppy again. One of the guys comes up and pokes his finger into my shoulder. He was trying to start on me. I just couldn't stop laughing.

As the smoke began to clear I could see Sid Byrne there

moving his finger around the spindle on the glass. Without taking his eyes off the break he shifted his side as Lou came rushing by, out into the car park. Then there was more movement behind. Gary and Dave sort of sandwiched Lou in a shoulder tackle from both sides as they overtook him. Lou spun and lost his balance on the loose stones. He put his hand down in a puddle to break the fall. Gary said sorry and helped him up and then did a legger again.

'Come on! Get fucking going!' Gary gripped my arm really tight. I was light in the head from laughing. I seemed to just get carried along.

We waited behind this skip outside the hairdresser's around the corner. It looked like they were in the middle of putting down some new lino. I made a mental note to come back after Christmas and tell them I could get a cheap deal for them down at the carpet shop. Gary and Dave were panting. I think I was breathless but I didn't notice. I was cracking myself. I couldn't keep it in. The look on everyone's faces. Dave looked like Han Solo when he got put in the carbon freeze. Gary was panicky and looking around. He's laid back, but he worries too much other times.

The others found us eventually. Paul had his arm around Esther like that bloke and that girl, and Carl was stumbling all over the place behind. Gary went 'Hey!' and they saw us.

'I . . . Jesus.' Paul didn't even look at me. I went off into the doorway of the hairdresser's. I just couldn't stop laughing. 'Where the fuck is he going now? What's he gonna do now?'

'Leave it. Just don't . . . say anything,' Gary goes.

I took in a deep breath and came back. I stood up straight and looked Paul in the eyes. No shame. There was no point.

Where was his sense of craic?

'Where's your sense of craic?'

'Don't say anything Paul. It's all right.'

'Yeah. We're gonna head now anyway. I'm just gonna walk Esther to the taxi and then I'm gonna head.'

'Are you not gonna give her a good Christmas ffff . . . Sorry. Sorry. Shit! Look! I've fucking boaked myself down my front. When did that fucking happen?!' Carl's mad.

'Yeah. Well anyway. We're gonna head.'

'Come back if you want after. We're going back to my gaff now to have a bit of blow,' Gary went on.

I was trying hard to keep it in but it was difficult. It was just so *funny*. Paul just looks at me again.

'Yeah. Well, we're gonna head.'

We seemed to lose Carl on the way home. I don't know where he fucked off to. He never even said, 'Merry Christmas.' Gary and Dave were on off ahead. I was trailing behind and Carl was off behind me again. I lost sight of him doing this thing we used to do in the rain, this snail-scotch we called it. You've got to make it all the way home by stamping on snails. You can't take a step unless you've got a snail to land on. There were millions of them. I tried to get Carl involved, but some of the bigger steps made him fall and stumble. I have decent balance even when I'm pissed. I got really into it and I was making good progress. It was amazing how much bigger my legs had grown in the years.

There's this clearness in your mind when you're pissed sometimes. The thing you're focusing on is the only thing that matters. '*One snail, two snail, three snail, four. Stamp! stamp! stamp! till we reach the front door.*'

*

When I got to the driveway Gary was standing there on his own.

'Where's Dave gone?' I asked.

'He went off home. I think he forgot it was Christmas.'

Gary opened the front door. There was a chill in the house. I was glad of it because I was still stewing.

'Shit anyway! I forgot to turn on the heat,' goes Gary.

'Here, what about this blow?'

'That was Dave's.'

'Oh. I think I have some upstairs myself. It's old but it's good stuff.'

'Nah, it's all right. I'm gonna hit the sack.' He was already on his way up the stairs.

I went in and stuck the kettle on. I made a cup of hot water to clean my mouth out. There was some sticky aftertaste like the aniseed had gone all weird or sour. It was like this coating in my mouth, or a film. It was like it was turning into something else, aniseedohol or testostrohol or somethingohol.

When the kettle stopped boiling I noticed the ringing then. Bubbling and silence and then . . . *Christ.*

Rrrrriiiing!!!!! Tiiiiiiiing!!!! Rrrrriiiing!!!!

This ringing in my ears. It was like a ringing in one ear and the noise of air being sucked out really fast in the other ear. The two of them were going in harmony, one over the other. For a couple of minutes my heart knocked out a rhythm that gave the noise this awful, panicky beat. When my pulse slowed down though the ringing just got louder. It was driving me mad. It was getting louder and louder. I couldn't get away from it. It was like a vacuum cleaner hoovering up dust in the groove that divides your brain. It was like a train.

I opened the fridge door then and that was better. I sunk where I sat in the wooden chair in the kitchen to the sound of the buzzing in the fridge. My hand hung down and I rubbed one of the rubbies. The rubbies stuck out like knees for the legs of the chair. They started off as weird old faces when the chair belonged to a Protestant church years ago, before we got it. I didn't have a dodie when I was younger and I used to suck on the rubbies instead. I ruined the value of what was probably the most valuable thing in the house by wearing down those faces by sucking at them. I never got grief off Da because I was too young. How can you tell a baby not to suck on something? You can't; it was my little thing then.

There were the rubbies and the sound of the fridge. It was just soothing. It soothed me off to sleep.

Soothe me Ma, Da. Soothe me, star light star bright.

Rrrrrrrrrrrrriiiiiiiiiiiiiiiiiiiiiiiiiiiiiiinnnnngggggggggg!!!!!!!!!!!!!!!!!!!!!
B a s t a r r r r r r r r r d d d !
Rrrrrrriiiiiiiiiinnnnnggggggggggg!!!!!!!!!!!!!!!!!!!

The Knight Rider clock said 5:23; these red digits in the darkness. I had to catch my breath. Gary forgot to say 'Merry Christmas.' I forgot too.

I thought about it. I thought about going up and saying 'Merry Christmas' then. Just shaking his shoulder and saying 'By the way . . .'

I didn't though. What the fuck did he mean by 'I forgot to turn on the heat'? What the fuck was all this 'I, I, I' business?

4

NINE

I walked through the hallway, into the kitchen and then into the TV room, and there was white all around, all pots of white paint lying on the floor. There was new fresh paint that hadn't quite dried yet up the walls. All white here, white there. White white. Plaster dust settled on the furniture that you could make a mark in with your finger, or in suspension in the air from sheets of plasterboard that Gary was cutting to shape with a Stanley knife. Blocks and sheets and pots of white. Everything was bleached and bright. Everything was in a bloody unnecessary mess.

There hadn't been much consultation on this one. This was my house too, and Gary had gone ahead and started with it. I shouldn't have stood idly by and let him charge ahead with this. I should have taken the reins the second he suggested we strip the house from top to bottom. I was against it from the very start. I didn't see that we should have touched the house. But the minute he got it into his brain, I should have taken over and shown him that I was as good as he was at this. There's nothing to this shit.

I went at the wallpaper pretty rapid at the start. That had been easy. That didn't count really. It came away like dead skin off the walls. You'd get the blade of the scraper under the paper just above the skirting board, slide it across a couple of inches so you'd have a nice flap you could get a handle on, give it a gentle hoist, and next thing the paper would just peel away in one go, from the floor to the smudges of damp rot at the top. I'd hold my breath as it came tumbling down so I wouldn't get the spores in my lungs.

It was really sad to see it go. I suppose it was a bit poncey with all the orange and brown flowers but it was sad all the same. If I hadn't gone at it though, Gary would have. It was part of the grand scheme. He wanted the place stripped of wallpaper and just bare paint up instead. He said it'd be easier to manage and it was more modern and you could just paint over any knocks or chips or greasy filth you couldn't scrub off. So I did most of the paper. But no. That had been easy. I wanted a go at the real work.

Gary was making a mess of the TV room. You could see it. It was an insulation job. The wall had been stripped down to the bare brickwork and there were scraps everywhere. Those hunks of plasterboard, big frayed candy-floss lumps of rolled-up glass fibre, wood splinters, nails all *over* the floor, sheets of breather paper chopped to fuck. And there was the wall staring at you, grey and rough, and not a tap done to it. Gary didn't know where to start. It was so obvious that someone had told him what to do and what to get, or he'd read it in a book or seen it on some TV show, and he'd gone out and spent hundreds of quid, and he'd ripped the wall down to its bare bones to make a start on it, and then he found he didn't know the first thing about what to do next. It was clear to me. I knew *exactly*.

First thing you've got to do is the breather paper. That has to be nailed up first before anything else is put on. You could see that Gary was getting the wooden battens ready first, but the breather paper has to be up on the wall before you lay on the battens. You put the paper up with clout nails, galvanized, the same things you use for roof felt. The most important thing to remember about the breather paper is that the side marked 'outside' should be facing out, so that it works properly by allowing moisture vapour in the wall to escape through the bricks and stops any damp that seeps through from the outside damaging the glass fibre. It's sort of a two-way thing. Then, and only then, once the breather paper is stuck up, do you nail on the battens. The battens make a wooden frame which gives the insulation material 'depth'. They make a space between the wall and the plasterboard so you can lay in the insulation material, which, in this case, was glass fibre. You fix the battens to the wall by drilling through the wood with a masonry bit into the brick, and then pushing a plug through each hole, and then tightening a screw into each plug in each hole. Once you have your frame, then it's on with the glass fibre, which you nail up like the breather paper with clout nails into the brickwork. Then you fix on the plasterboard, cut to measure so that each section is the width of the span from one batten to the next, and you nail these to the wood and try not to leave too big a gap between sections. You don't want too big a crack here because it's important to have a smooth enough surface for when the plaster goes on. The plaster will smooth over any big blemishes or holes and shit anyway, but having a nice even surface will make the job easier. The best thing actually is to get a professional to do the plastering, but the other shit's easy.

Gary was all on about this insulating because the TV room

was up against the outer wall, on the side of the house that was most exposed to the rain. Apparently, loads of other houses on the road had been having problems with the same side and people were doing this insulation business that the original builders forgot to take care of back in the sixties.

The other room lying up against the outer wall on that side was directly above, in Da's room. Gary had been going on about doing up the room and getting in some students for a bit of extra cash.

The top of the stairs was cluttered up with shit moved out of Da's room. It had been blocking up the landing for two days, but I hadn't really stopped to look around. I'd had to squeeze by Da's huge double bed up on its side and the mattress up against that as it lay at an angle on to it like a lean-to. Da needed the double bed so he could sleep diagonally. The smell of his BO was still soaked into the bed. You'd get it as you shuffled by. It was seeped right into the mattress and through into the bed itself and into the lace around the side which was all creamy and off-white, like the colour of the inside of Magnums. The sweat came down in marks like caramel melting.

I noticed all these boxes around the back of the bed. Gary had been clearing stuff out of Da's room and putting them in boxes.

Da's room was nearly in the same state as the TV room except that Gary had painted three of the walls with that squinty white. The other wall was the same as the one downstairs, stripped and all grey-ish brick. The floor was covered with the same sort of mess as the TV room too.

There was something about the room now though, despite

the clutter. I'd never seen anything look so bare and empty. It was unrecognizable from before. The shelves with Da's books and tapes were gone and even the mark where they would have been screwed against the wall was painted over. The one or two pictures – the copper scratching thing with Nelson's Pillar and that drawing of the seafront in Bray – were all gone too. Everything was obliterated and gone and packaged away in boxes.

And then there were all these holes. Three holes about an inch wide drilled right through the brick into the outside so that the daylight came through. What is this for? I thought. Ventilation? Peepholes?

I picked up the hammer drill that Gary had hired. It was still plugged in even though it had been resting in its box. I gave it a firm squeeze on the trigger and it let out these sharp shuddery blows and the long masonry bit shot in and out in the air at the same time as it rotated. It gave out the scream of grinding concrete like it was summoning up the ghosts of old walls. I put it back in the case and then I looked at the bare brick wall.

Right, I was thinking. Let's get cracking on this. A sheet of breather paper, a bunch of clout nails – let's get moving with this. Up with the paper, pressed up on the brick, the nail held steady between your thumb and your finger, bang with the hammer, bang bang. Bang bang . . .

It was harder going than I thought though. You really needed two people.

You actually do notice the drop in temperature as the sun goes down. It's weird. The temperature goes down as the shadows move and the light fades. You only notice it if you stay still in the one spot for hours and concentrate on it. There's a noticeable drop. It was getting quite chilly. I lifted my head. The hair on the back was covered in plaster dust.

Gary hadn't come home yet. He'd been out with Dave and Carl for the day. I looked around the room. Everything was lying around as it was when I came in. The wall facing me was still bare and grey and a sheet of breather paper was lying over my legs, pinned to the bottom of the wall with two clout nails. A length of batten was balancing on my belly. Both ends were gently see-sawing in the air as I breathed. It hadn't touched the floor in hours. I'd managed to keep it at its centre of gravity over all this time; amazing.

I threw the batten aside and got up and stretched myself. I went over and flicked on the light. I looked around the room again. *No work done.* I went over to the hammer drill and gave it another go in mid-air. *No work done.* No work done and how *dare* Gary. *How fucking dare he!* I threw the drill back into its box again. How dare he! This room was never meant to be white. I couldn't do anything about it though. What could I do? I'd tried and what could I do? I picked up the drill again. *Right so.* Time to bring some of this crashing down. If I can't do anything, I'll bring him down to my level. I'll bring them all down to my level, by God I will.

TEN

Any way I moved I couldn't escape from the sound of the springs. The slightest twitch to the left or to the right and they'd start off again. It could have grated if I'd allowed it. But I let it become part of this little world I'd set down in. It was the soundtrack. It was something magical. It was like the sound of depression and silence. It was the sound of a bell falling from its rotten rope through a tower in a town in some valley. If I put my head down on the mattress, beneath the pillows, right down flat, I could hear it. Listen, listen. It was the sound of a million tuning forks tingling in a far-away lab. It was like a rat in a radiator or an axe on an organ.

There was another sound. *Knock, knock, tickety-tick. Whirr-r-r-r.* The bangs and scrapes of all the DIY and home improvement eventually stopped after a whole morning. I could hear Gary stirring in the kitchen. He hung around there for a while; I could hear the kettle bubbling and flick itself off, the creak of one of the chairs perched back on its hind legs. In the silence I could hear him ticking things over in his mind. Then the kitchen door swung open. I could hear him thinking to himself, going, 'Right, this is ridiculous, this is so ridiculous.' Ha! Dick! Was he going to climb the stairs? It was hard to tell until the second-last step. The builders had done such a good job on our stairs they could have been made of stone. But there was that loose floor board on the second-last step. It bent under the weight of a foot and made a noise. I tensed myself rigid in the bed for the confrontation. I sat up slightly. But Gary stopped dead outside the door. He'd learned his lesson from the last time.

'Jer, are you gonna have some lunch?'

'No.'

'Okay. Have you even had breakfast?'

I didn't answer. I heard his hand on the door handle.

'Get away from there! I'm fucking telling you! Don't take a step closer.'

'All right, all right. I wasn't going to do anything. Look, Jer, have you had any breakfast this morning?'

'Yes. I went down really early. I brought it back up.'

He didn't say anything for a minute.

'What do you mean now, "brought it back up"? Brought it back up to bed or brought . . .'

'Yes! Brought it back up to bed.'

There was another minute of quiet.

'Jer, y'know . . . it's Thursday.'

'I know that. Shouldn't you be at work so?'

'No. I've the day off. But you should be at school. I know that.'

'Don't fucking get smart with me! I'll get up and box you out of it!'

'Good. Do that. It might get you up and about then.'

He disappeared down the stairs again, and shouted back up: 'It's Thursday. Come on. This is ridiculous.'

Thursday, so. Really? Shit. Ah well. Thursday. This had

gone on since Sunday. Or really Saturday night. I went to bed
on Saturday and never got up on Sunday morning. On then
on into Monday, Tuesday, then into Wednesday. I could have
sworn it was still Wednesday. Or maybe Friday. The days
turned into a bit of a mush after Monday. Thursday, so.

I'd had a bit of a close shave with a car again. I was crossing
a road with my Walkman on. I got confused because it was a
T-junction. I got mixed up about which way to look. I sometimes don't know my left from my right anyway. I have to
think really hard about it. If a teacher asks me to lift my right
arm, I'll lift my left arm. I was getting really into this song. It
was my favourite album, Blur, *Parklife*, and 'Jubilee' was on. I
was imagining I was up on the stage, like that bloke, giving it
loads. There's this line, 'Hey mister tax collecter, don't pick on
me, I'm on-ly, seven-teen!' I was gritting my teeth, mouthing
it, miming, as I crossed the road. I might as well have had my
eyes shut; I was on a different planet. I didn't even hear the
brakes. When I looked to my right there was a car about 3
inches away. The driver jumped out and slammed the door in
one movement. He was absolutely livid. Livid. He started to
twirl his fingers around his ears and shout at me. I couldn't
make out a word. The volume was up full blast. I took the
headphones out of my ears to listen. I knew then that he'd
been gesturing for me to take the headphones out of my ears
to listen.

'You dozy bloody idiot! I could've killed you! You could've
been killed and no one could've saved you! What would you
have done then? Huh? You would've been stone dead and it'd
be too late! I could be scraping you up off the street by now!
Idiot!'

I'd been thinking about that a lot. There's so much out there that could blow you out like a match.

Then on the Friday before, I went out for a walk in the evening. I didn't bring my Walkman, and I stayed close to the paths and tight to the hedges. I tried to take the route down the estate, through the next estate and then back up the main road and around the block back home again that would leave me needing to cross the least amount of roads. Within half a mile I was panting and I didn't know why. All I knew was that I needed to find my way back to the house again. I needed to take the direct route back; back from where I came. I stopped outside somebody's gate to calm down a little and get my bearings. I lit up a fag and took in a few gulps deep and slow.

The light from up the driveway drew me. It was streaming out of the window of the living room, this huge window with the curtains open and pegged back; warm, golden light, dancing with the flicker of this real coal fire. I hadn't seen one of those before ever. Not in any of the houses in our area. We all had the space in the wall and the chimney, but most people had it filled in with reproduction electric or gas fires. I moved closer to take a look and to push my cheek against the glass because I was sure that the fire would heat up the window; it looked that warm. I saw also that the largest shadow in the room, the one that was jumping about past the flower bed and into the front garden, was made by two little girls playing in the room. There was Lego and shit, that's what one of them was playing with, and the other girl had some sort of chewed-up figure and was lifting it in and out of a kind of enclosure that her sister had made from mainly green and black bricks. I went right up to the window sill to get a closer look and stood there with my hands in my pockets. I breathed out on the glass and it formed all condensation. I put my nose up to it and I was surprised to feel the coldness. One of the girls looked up.

'Ahhhhh! Da! Da! Get Da! The man! Look! Help! The man!'

The screams came right through the window, so high-pitched I was convinced the glass would shatter. I thought it might cave in on me so I took a step back and fell into some muck and roses. I gathered myself up but I decided to stay where I was. If I ran now it would look extra-dodgy; I'd look like a kiddy fiddler. I stayed put right in the flower bed and told myself to look the Da in the eyes when he came out and state my case. I heard the front door open and close with a wallop at the side.

'You little fucking sicko!'

'I . . .'

'What the fuck are you doing?!'

'M . . .'

'What the fuck are your hands doing in your pockets?!'

'Uh . . .'

'And get the fuck out of my roses!'

'Yes.'

He made me feel like a filthy, oily animal. I couldn't get rid of the feeling of guilt for no reason and stupidity all through the following day, the Saturday. By about teatime though I'd forgotten about it. But I still went to bed and didn't get up.

One of the days while I was drifting off in the middle of the afternoon, I had this dream. They'd locked me up in this old castle on a hill, where the earth and rocks rose up in all curves to join the base of the tower like a root. There were guards with dull, metal helmets with designs on them covering their faces patrolling the corridor outside past the door of my cell. They were dragging prisoners out of cells, day by day, one by one, and throwing them down this hole. Any day now I knew it would be my turn to fall into the boiling tar. But I wasn't going to allow it to happen. No, no. I'm Jerome Morris and I wasn't going to allow this to happen. Unlike the other prisoners, I still had some fat between my ribs and my hair was thick on my head; I'd been one of the few to escape the shaving for head lice. I still had a powerful big strong set of elbows. I was going to crawl to freedom. Out past the rusty grille in my cell, through the slime in the damp stone air vent and towards the light. When I kicked out the grille at the other end I was almost blinded with the volume and intensity of this white, bright, lovely light. And as my eyes adjusted, the contrast all settled, and everything looked clear. I could see for miles and miles, from up here, 200 feet up, out of this little gap in the side of this sheer wall in the tower on the hill, looking out over this massive plain, with all the little villages and rivers catching the sun, out beyond the horizon to somewhere in the direction of home. Home. That was all I needed to keep me going. The idea that somewhere out there in that direction was my Home. I thought of Home as I scaled the brickwork, across first, past some loopholes, and then down about a hundred feet. I jumped the rest and the thought of Home numbed the smack on my feet as I landed. And all the way as I rolled down the bank of earth and swam the moat and jumped a ditch from another bank of earth and climbed another wall and jumped that too I thought of it. Home. Home. I followed the rivers as they flowed into each other and hid under bridges as patrols went overhead looking for me and I huddled there and thought of it then. I thought of Home as I slept in a forest and ate a bat on a spit on a fire. I ran through a bog and a dust bowl and past a 9-inch nail factory where they made spikes for the torture devices in the castle and thought of it all the way. Take me Home, Home, take me Home.

But then I woke and the reality hit me like one of those iron hands of one of the prison-guards reaching out from my dream and striking me across the temple. Home was a house with a real coal fire and this house was just a shell.

Reality. The best way to beat your fears is to face up to them. I knew this. All the real things outside my door. There's so much sadness and danger in the world and you can't move for the way it blocks up the streets like the ghosts of people who've dropped dead on every square inch of the path. These real things. I had to face them like I'd faced my real fears before.

I'd been through it before once, I remembered. It was on a school trip in first year. We went down on some shitty arts and crafts trip for a few days in some old country farmhouse, this huge big thing with vaults and servants' quarters. The highlight of the trip for everyone was soon revealed, and it wasn't a play or a potter's wheel or a St Brigid's Cross workshop. A massive spider was living in the dorm above everyone's heads. It was so huge it looked like a little black dog had got up and learned how to defy gravity. For the next few days, boys were all pointing and sniggering and girls were screaming. There were hands running up backs and skirts and tops of mops were left in beds. The whole trip centred around that spider, and I was terrified but I didn't tell anyone. It was my biggest phobia, ever since I was a baby, for as long as I could remember, ever since I became aware of my surroundings and the things that crawled out of shadows and secret hiding places and Da's hairy fingers. I made excuses to swap beds with someone on the other side of the dorm – something like I needed to be near a window for air – and even still I sweated myself wet every night.

Then on the last night I went to the toilet in the middle of the night and I flicked on the light in the old yellow bathroom. In the corner of my eye I caught a black flash by the sink. My heart dropped a foot into my bowels. I turned to face the speck of whatever it was and saw it was the spider and found that if I faced the source of the fear before the initial fright had time to settle then it wasn't so bad. The electricity just consumes you and you don't have time to think too hard about it and collapse in relief and allow the adrenalin to flow out and drain you dead. I went up closer and closer, tempting myself, not questioning what I was doing. It was huge all right – the biggest spider I'd ever seen. It had probably been there in the house for centuries, grown huge on all smoke from peat and potato steam. Big bony legs with knuckles and webbed leather between the thighs and body. Trouty speckles all over its back. The skin stretched and relaxed as it breathed in and out. I'd imagined it had been given a name hundreds of years ago; I'd imagined it had been christened 'Bran' and it had a place on the family crest. I stretched out my hand and touched it and it came alive. It ran across the back of the sink and changed the light in the room, it was so huge. Then it stopped and rested at the edge. I threw both my hands out again and clasped it, and it danced like Irish dancing between my palms, tickling them like feathers. I brought it out to my bed in the dorm and put it in a Thermos flask for the next morning. It was still alive and well and stretching its skin with its breathing and getting all fat on drops of milky tea when I checked on it before breakfast. The jolt of courage had lodged in me, no question, and hadn't got lost in the night. I was jubilant. I had conquered my fear of spiders by facing up to it, facing up to the biggest fat mother of them all and staring into its eight ugly eyes. I closed the lid on the flask again and ran out to the theatre area in the house and I got a crumpled top hat, a cape and a pair of pointy shoes. I went back out to the dorm and the bed and the spider again and held Bran with one hand this time, while I twiddled the fingers of my other hand and leapt around and frightened girls. Then the teacher came in and whipped the top hat off and clattered me one and crushed the spider with his boot. But I had faced up to my fear.

And that's what I decided to do with this new fear. I just got up and faced the light again; that's what got me out of bed. That and this piece I'd remembered reading in a magazine about how faulty bed springs are the fifth biggest killer in America or something.

I made myself go back to school on the Friday. Another short, sharp dose of reality, quick and now; there was no point in putting it off. So I lumbered and I pushed on, all little slow steps, dum dum dum, a real effort. When I got to the gates I could feel a something ghost through my body. This pounding and thumping, this something cutting the air, surging through my chest, *dooosh*. It was coming from the direction of the

yard. Inside, this big gang of lads were knocking a tennis ball
about. It was pinging around like pin-ball. The height of the
walls produced sharp watery swimming-pool echoes and the
cold air carried the sound waves. The open door of one of the
bike sheds was the goal at one end and a couple of jackets
down by the bunker was the other. It was about twenty-a-side,
with a few girls joining in, messing, or just hanging around the
edge.

I slipped down by the bike racks to get to the side doors of
H-block with the least amount of fuss. I looked up for a
second and realized I shouldn't have worried. Nobody really
noticed or cared. I continued on.

But then suddenly there were forty sets of eyes on me. I
glanced to my left and the ball was coming down in my direction after a freak bounce. Everyone was frozen in whatever
position they were in when the last kick was made. Everyone
was anticipating what I'd do. As much to look away from the
staring as anything, I focused up into the air at the ball dropping and dropping as it came closer to me. Then, without
needing even to think, I turned up my foot and trapped the
ball brilliantly on the instep, giving it just enough recoil so it
wouldn't rebound. It made a beautiful pat as my foot took the
whip out of it. Ah yes. This was perfect. *Poetry.* There were
girls there, girls all around. I realized I was fulfilling a dream
I'd had loads of times before.

The next step was to weave past ten defenders and then
walk the ball into the net or else crash in a scorcher from 30
yards. I set out on the foray and slipped by my first man like
an eel. The soles of my shoes were making lovely pep-pepper-
ing sounds on the concrete as my feet feinted and made

dummy movements around the ball. Another man fell aside. This was working out so well. Another man left for dead. So well. I didn't think my return to school would start out so well. I was dreading this and then . . . this. Another man. Another. Another . . . Another . . . Another . . . Another . . . the leg back and . . . *whack!*

I should have kept my head down for the follow-through. The ball sliced viciously to the right and clanged off the shutter on the tuck shop. The thin metal sheeting rippled like waves on a pond. When I looked back I could see them all standing there with their hands on their hips. They hadn't made any effort. It wasn't an awe thing. They just hadn't made any effort and they were standing around making gozzies and sniggering about me.

Peter English had his own view on it. He squirted this stream of all chocolatey spit from the gap between his front teeth.

'Morris.'

I didn't say anything. I put my bag down on the ground. I sat down on a bollard and fiddled with my shoe.

'Morris.'

I didn't say anything.

'Morris. Hm. Morris. The "back to school boy". I don't remember you being sent for off the bench.'

'Ah well. Y'know . . .'

'I don't remember you getting a place on the bench at all. Just fuck off. We weren't actually playing with you there. Every single one of us out there was just standing thinking, looking, thinking you're some fucking retard shit.'

'Ah I know that. But the lads . . .'

'The "*lads!*' D'you hear this? The lads! The lads don't like you. The lads hate you. *I* hate you. I *hate* you. We all think you're a faggot. *Faggot!*'

'I'm not a *fucking* faggot. I had a bird for a good while.'

A bunch of Peter English's mates started laughing.

'You are. You're a faggot.'

'I'm not. I had a bird.'

'Oh no, no. You are. You misunderstand me. You are. You're a faggot.'

'But I'm not. I used to have a bird.'

'Doesn't make a difference. You're a faggot.'

'I'm not.'

'Faggot!'

'I had a bird.'

'Doesn't matter. Faggot's a faggot. *Faggot!*'

It was nine o'clock and the bell went off. Slowly, everyone made their way towards the side doors. As the lads around the bunker joined the surge, this rocket comes my way. The ball zoomed past my head, missing me by an inch, shot into an empty bike rack, bounced around inside the bracket for a second, flew out again, and I caught it, and I threw it back gently along the ground. James Ryan, one of Peter English's good mates, still had his foot up in the air, and there was this sneer on his face.

Friday mornings really should have been a killer with Powell and Irish, but as was normal recently, I knew I could sit around and do nothing and get away with it. Powell was spouting his usual shit. For some reason today he had a framed picture of somebody famous hung up just under the cross of Jesus. It was a side profile. Sort of a bulby nose and going a bit bald. I knew it was one of the 1916 people but I wasn't sure exactly who. Either Pearse or Connolly or one of those.

'Anois. "Tréithe An Phiarsaigh". An bhfuil fhios agat cad atá i gceist agam nuair a deirim "tréithe"?'

A beautiful smell of creosote was coming up from the field. Hannon the odd-job man was slumping around with a wheel marking the lines of an athletics track on the grass. The lovely chemical smell wafted in through the open window from the miles of lines already laid down. It was weird the way the window had to be left open with the heat. It wasn't a warm day at all outside but the double-glazing blocked out the breeze and left only the sun. You can't feel the sun in February unless you're inside and there's glass between you and it. Then it could be a hot day in July as it gets intensified and sears.

'. . . I 1908, sásaigh Piarsaigh uaillmhian mór nuair a bhunaigh sé scoil dá-theangach Naomh Éanna i Raghnallach. Níos deanaí, d'aistritear suíomh na scoile go Ráth Fearnáin . . .'

The sun in the sky in the winter isn't a source of heat. It only draws attention to the bitter, clear sky and lights up the little particles of ice here and there on the ground and the little bits of frost and shows up just how cold it is. But the sun in the sky in the winter is the clearest sun of all. The sun in the sky in the summer melts into the dust high up and it's hard to make it out in the haze and the blur. The sun in the sky in the winter is as clear and as fresh as the sky around it. But this isn't the sun in the sky in winter, I thought. This is the sun in the sky in the spring. This is the sun in the sky in late February. It was late February already and I hadn't even noticed it creep up.

'. . . Anois, más féidir libh bhur cóipleabhair a oscailt agus cleachtadh beag a thósú dom . . .'

I found myself doodling chimneys with a leaky biro on the cover of my foolscap pad. Scratchy black industrial chimneys, fat in the middle like cartoon cigars and churning out thick smoke. Powell was on his patrol around the classroom as everyone had their heads down working away. He was making his way up the second-last aisle to the top of the row of desks beside me, and down the window aisle. I wasn't worried. He'd catch me doing nothing but he wouldn't say anything. I started looking for an old passport photo of myself in my pencil case that I scribbled over years ago with a funny face with a beard and glasses.

'*An dtuigeann tú cad atá i gceist leis an cleachtadh seo, a Uasal Morris?*'

Powell put his big deformed hands down resting on the head of my desk. They were two big yellow hands, with the fingers curled inwards so they looked like the paws of a tiger. He whispered loudly again.

'*An dtuigeann tú cad atá le dhéanamh? An bhfuil cabhair ag teastáil uait?*'

He got down on his hunkers and put his face level with mine. His arm was lying along the back of my seat.

'*Deirfeidh mé é seo as Béarla, lé go gcuireann sé as go mór liom.* Do you understand what I'm asking you to do here, Jerome? It's not too difficult. I only want about a hundred and fifty words.'

'I do understand, yeah. I'm getting down to it now,' I said, hoping that he'd go away and leave me to it. But he just waited there and watched as I wriggled in my seat. I had no idea where to look. He watched me as I coloured in an 'O' in my book.

'Are you feeling any better, Jerome?'

'Yes. No. Yes. I mean, yes.'

'I mean, are you feeling better after your lay-off during the week?'

'Yeah, I am. Thanks.'

'Was it this flu that's going around?'

'It was, yeah.'

'Oh, it's a terrible old thing. I'd better keep away from you so.'

He kept his face right down level with me.

'And would you not have thought about getting in touch on one of the days? I can tell you now that we had a big discussion in the staffroom yesterday concerning your whereabouts.'

'I thought about it.'

'You thought about it?'

'I thought about it but I didn't.'

'Right. Well, in lieu of a phone call then, have you a letter for me?'

'No I don't.'

'You do know that as the head teacher for this year, all doctors' or guardians' letters should be handed to me?'

'Yes I know, but I don't have a letter. Who should I have got to write it?'

'*Who sh . . .?* Oh. Right. Okay. Sorry.' The hand moved from the back of the seat and he put it on my shoulder. 'Who is your guardian now? Whoever is your guardian should have written the letter.'

'I don't have a guardian.'

'You have an older brother, don't you?'

'He's not my guardian.'

'Jerome, we're only ever concerned for you. That's why we

want the letter. We're not out to get at pupils. We need a letter for form's sake, for the roll.'

'Well I don't have one.'

'Right. Okay. You don't have one.'

'I don't have one so stop asking.'

'*Gabh mo leithscéal?*'

'I don't have one so stop asking and stop going on about it. You're wrecking my head.'

'Jerome . . .'

'You're wrecking my fucking head.'

'Jerome! *J*. . .! Now, come on now. This is not on! This is an unacceptable way to talk to a teacher.' Powell raised his voice so the whole class could hear. 'Say sorry immediately!'

I kept quiet.

'Jerome, apologize immediately,' Powell was still shouting to the class, 'and I won't punish you.'

I stood up.

'What? No! Sit down! Say sorry! Apologize!'

I stayed standing and wobbled from side to side and looked down at my desk. I bit my lip while I thought about something. I thought about the words to say.

'Jerome, come on now. Say you're sorry now and we won't bring you down to Mr Nagle.'

Then I looked up.

'Patrick Pearse is a queer and I didn't ring up during the week because I fucking hate the kip and if I did I would only have rung to tell you that you're all cunts and I fucking hate you and Patrick Pearse is a faggot and I hate Irish and it's a shit language and I don't have a letter and if I did I would have wiped my arse with it.'

The classroom exploded with laughter. Everyone tried to muzzle themselves as Powell swung around waving wildly. Then he turned back to me. He got calm again.

'Jerome. Come down with me now to Mr Nagle's office.'

I gave the class the thumbs-up behind Powell's back as I left the room. Powell brought me down the corridor with his hand resting on my shoulder. He didn't say anything until we reached Mr Nagle's – The Taoiseach's – office.

The Taoiseach's office was divided into two sections. There was the bit just inside the doorway where there was no door where Miss Agnew the secretary's desk was and then there was the main bit where The Taoiseach had his desk.

'*Ah! Dia dhuit, a mháistir!*'

The Taoiseach had a few words with me about shit in the first section and then disappeared behind the door with Powell. I could hear the two of them speak in Irish behind the glass. I sat down on a seat across from Miss Agnew and I could hear them talk about me but I couldn't understand. Miss Agnew was tapping away at her computer and glancing up at me every so often.

'Jerome Morris, isn't it?'

'Yeah.'

'What are you down here for, Jerome?'

'Ah, I'm just in some trouble with Powell and The Taoiseach.'

'Sshhh!' she hushed, and held her finger up to her lips and sank her head into her shoulders and giggled. 'Don't let anyone around here hear you say *that*!'

She kept giggling.

'I'm sorry,' I said, 'It's just a bit of a nickname.'

She went on typing, then said after a second: 'Our one's worse.'

'Your what?'

'Our nickname's worse. The nickname the staff have for Mr Nagle.'

'What is it?'

'I better not say. If it got around . . .'

Miss Agnew looked quite young. She couldn't have been more than ten years older than me. She was nice looking. She was nice and she was nice looking.

'Ah, go on. What is it?'

'You're not to say anything to anyone, okay?' she glanced really quickly over at the door into where The Taoiseach was. '*Marbles*.'

'Marbles?'

'Yeah. Mr Cleland thought of it.'

'Why do you call him that?'

'Well, see up at the glass there, where the letters are?' she pointed to where seven stickers spelling 'MR NAGLE' were stuck on the inside of the glass on the partition, like a cop in a film's office. 'See the way they spell out 'ELGAN' from this side?'

'Em. No. Not really.'

'Well obviously the letters are backwards from here. They're in – this is Mr Cleland who spotted this now, not me – they're in mirror image. But they actually do spell 'ELGAN' if you ignore them being backwards. See?'

'And what's that got to do with The Taoiseach being called "Marbles" then?'

'Well, ELGAN, as in the Elgin Marbles. They're some

diamonds in Scotland or something. I dunno. Mr Cleland thought of it. The name's stuck though.'

'Marbles. Yeah. Good one. I like it. It's like he lost his marbles. *Marbles.*'

'Now remember, Jerome – not a word. Seriously.'

'Not a word,' I said, and we both giggled.

The name suited. When I looked at Mr Nagle come out of the office with Powell I could see. *Marbles.* There was something about the way his forehead looked all pale and the veins. Some names just suit some people.

'Jerome,' Marbles started, 'Mr Powell has been telling me all that happened in class. This is a very serious breach of conduct, do you understand?'

I pretended to look all ashamed and nodded.

'Cursing in class is just about as serious as it gets by our rules. And then cursing at a teacher . . . And sexual swearwords in front of girls. This was an attack. We just can't have it.'

They both stood there almost shoulder-to-shoulder, almost cheek-to-cheek, peering at me like I'm this goldfish in a bowl.

'Now, Jerome. I appreciate how difficult, how awful, it's been for you, how really hard it must be at home. But we really can't be having this sort of behaviour in class. What sort of example do you think we'd be setting to the rest of your year if we let you off the hook on this one? And if word got around to, say, the *first* years, what sort of example would we be setting them if we didn't censure you properly?'

Miss Agnew was working away at her computer. I wanted her to say something. I wanted her to stick up for me and I wanted to hear her nice voice reassure me.

'No. I'm afraid, Jerome, that we can't let this one drop. This is serious stuff indeed. We have no option in this case but to implement the full force of school discipline. Four days' suspension, effective from today.'

Powell shook his head and tut-tutted. Actually, he looked kind of sorry.

'Well really, a five-day suspension. Because we don't want to see you until next Friday.'

I stared at Miss Agnew. I hoped to catch her attention by looking at her hard enough. I wanted her to look up from her screen and give me a smile. She was just being a fucking robot now.

'No actually, finish up your classes today, then go home and don't come in Monday to Thursday inclusive next week. So, four days then.'

I made for the door and looked back again at Miss Agnew. I wanted so bad for her to just lift her head and give me a wink and a smile. A wink would make everything seem all right.

'So back to class then, Jerome, and then don't come back till next Friday morning. I'm sorry, but it's got to be done. We have to abide by the rules.'

But I didn't go back to class. While Powell and Mr Nagle continued talking in the office for a while, I slipped out the doors and headed home. And I got more and more depressed the longer I walked, the more I thought about shit.

ELEVEN

What's really going to hurt the cunt, I asked myself? If there's one thing in the house I could beat him to a pulp with and let him know I meant business with and let him know who's boss with, what is it? I took up one of the battens in my hand, one of the ones he was using to make such a mess of the TV room and Da's room. All this shit was driving me mad. He was really charging ahead with it now. The plasterboard was up in the TV room and most of the glass fibre was up in Da's room. He'd taken a bit of a break with both those rooms after he stripped down the walls, and he'd completely overhauled the kitchen in the meanwhile. All the presses had been cleared out of shit, the extractor fan had been taken down and the muck cleaned out the back, the old carpet had been pulled up and all the walls and the ceiling had been painted. Then he went back to the TV room and Da's room and threw up the insulation on the walls.

I tested the piece of batten in my hands. No. Not springy enough. It could break over his back with one good whack. I needed something I could keep on hitting and hitting him with.

I found this thing eventually. A section of yellow plastic track, with a red slat at one end, and a slit in the other – a slat and a slit – and we used to lock all these sections together to make a big curly loop-the-loop and a ramp and a run-up, and we'd shoot Matchbox cars up it. I held the two ends between the palms of my hands and squeezed my arms together. The section would almost make a fully closed oval with the ends nearly touching before a crease of white would form across the exact middle of the track and you knew you had to let it spring back before the plastic might bend beyond repair. Just supple enough.

I hid in the cupboard under the stairs and waited. I pressed the light in my digital watch and it said it was quarter to seven. Gary would be home soon. I sat back against the wall that didn't have the slope above it and left the door slightly ajar. I tucked into a big bag of different-flavoured packets of crisps and a can of Foster's and then I lit a fag. I kept kissing the plastic of the track.

The splutter of Gary's banjaxed engine came slowly up the driveway. It wasn't that dark, but he was flicking his headlights on and off in the gloom of the car port and I could see the light through the gap where the door of the cupboard was open. It was streaming through the frosted glass beside the front door and lit up the hallway, and then the noise of the engine stopped and the lights went off for good.

I got up into a squat as the Chubb fumbled in the lock. The door opened and then closed. I struck the piece of track against one of my own palms. *Pat, pat.* Just the job, I was thinking. There was the creak of leather as he hung his jacket up on the coat rack, the swivel of his soles on the carpet, one step, two step, three step, *come on, come on,* four step, up to the cupboard door, *come on cunt, into the kitchen you go,* five step, past the doorway now, and . . .

'Jer! Wait till you hear . . .!'

. . . Right! I'm gonna kill the bastard!

ATTACK! ATTACK! ATTACK!

HASSS-*AAWWWW!* With one kick, the door flew open. HAIIIEEE-*YAAAH!* I sprung up off my hunkers like a grasshopper and on to the balls of my feet with my legs wide apart. Gary turned around and looked at me all startled.

'Jer, what the fuck . . .?!'

HAIIIEEE-*YEEEH!* With a sideways slash from over my head, I cracked the track into his forehead. He grabbed his face and squealed and bent over in pain. HAIIIEEE-YAKKA-TAKKA-*TAKKA!* I came down hard with another stroke, aiming for a little black mole on the back of his neck.

KATANGA-TANGA-TANGA-*TANGAAAAAH!* And again, and again, and again, and again! With each whoosh you could hear the air rushing and crashing around the blade as if it was breaking the speed of sound. Into the fucking ground, cunt! Into the fucking ground! Smack and sting!

Gary was on his knees and protecting his head with his arms. I stopped and waited for a sound. He looked for a second all frightened through the gap in the 'V' of his arm.

One more for good measure then . . .

FFFFFUT-*ANNGGG!*

. . . and then I threw the track aside and ran out the front door.

And I ran and I ran and I didn't need to go back to the house because I had everything I needed in my pockets. The Solpadeine and the Aller-eze and the painkillers for Da's cancer and the little container of steroids. I could hear them rattle as I ran.

And I ran down out of our estate and through the green and through slasher's lane and through the jungle and out by the footbridge and across the dualler to the church, the best place, the proper place to do this. I blessed myself before I went inside because I wasn't taking any chances that there was no God. Not at this time. I had to go through that whole proce-dure just in case.

I wasn't scared or anything. I just had this feeling that things had to be cleared up before I went off. Normally the church would have freaked me out a bit. I remembered the scaredy feeling from being brought to mass the odd time at Christmas or for school masses or when Da died. The smell of wax and pine everywhere, it'd make you sick. But I was just focused on the task. I had to take out my insurance for my trip if there was to be one. I made my way to the best place to do it, this thing that'd catch the corner of my eye any time I had been here, this thing that'd *really* freak me out, that I'd try to not look at, but your eyes would just be drawn. When I looked at it now, it was pretty deadly. This angel, who I think was St Michael, the archangel, was standing up over the Devil. He was only just about looking down at him – his head was straight up but his eyes were kind of half-way turned down, all snooty – and the Devil was lying there, the look of agony on his face, his arms spread out like Jesus, and blood pumping out of his chest as St Michael jabbed a huge fork into him to kill him. It was all painted in these dark hundred-year-old paints that were shiny there in the alcove behind the wooden rail. I knelt down on the pad and laid out the tablets and the other things where people usually put their handbags. I blessed myself again and put my elbows up on the rail and thought, right, a couple of minutes; a couple of minutes now to clear the decks; that should do it.

There was this other old bloke there and the outside corners of his eyes were scrunched up all leathery. His lips were moving but you couldn't properly hear what he was saying, just this sort of soft whispy whistle every so often when he hit the 'T's or the 'S's in his prayer. He was putting me off with the noise. It was like that really annoying Anto whistle that people do over the tip of their tongue through their teeth. I couldn't compose myself for my prayer. I tried to think of something else for a second so that I could focus on another thing and then the prayer inside would be just drawn out, like a magic-eye picture in my mind. I started laughing then for some reason. I can't remember what shit I was thinking about, but I just started laughing and giggling to myself. When I looked over again at the guy he'd gone.

Oh Hail Mary ace of spades, is the Lord with thee? I started going to myself. *Blessed is the fruit of thee against women and pray for us sinners, and pray for us now in the hour of our bed and* . . .

It had been so long though, shit. And it was like, if you don't get the right code you won't get through, and I *knew* that, but I couldn't think of the basics. I tried the other one, the *Our Father*, but that was even more difficult. There were more words. I preferred the *Hail Mary* anyway because it seemed softer and nicer because there was a woman in it who'd be more caring rather than this harsh, strict father with a beard.

I looked down at the medicines on the shelf. Jesus. The realization. This was it. Nineteen eighty something to nineteen ninety . . .

I thought of my confirmation photo suddenly. Just the picture of me with the brown background and what I always thought was an alien cloud behind but was actually only a special mark on the card to highlight me on my very special day.

I started crying when I thought of it. I hadn't cried in months and months. I used to have a smile on my face back then, back when I didn't think about any shit going on around me. I used to cry all the time then, even though I was happy. I hadn't cried in the last few months, even though it was sort of a funny feeling. I don't know. The last couple of months had just been weird. I didn't go around smiling, but I'd never cried all the same. Here I was now blubbing. I was crying because of all these things and because of the smile. Just the image of it.

My head was full of this ball of pain from trying to control the crying. I hadn't wanted to draw attention to myself in case anyone came over and twigged what I was up to. I put my hands together like that 'this is a church and this is the steeple' and then opened my hands out and held them above my eyes like a visor and rubbed my temples with my thumbs. It helped clear my head a bit. Then I looked up again at the statue of St Michael. I clenched my hands together tighter and kept on looking. I looked and I thought and clenching my hands together helped me to think. If you looked at St Michael's eyes he wasn't looking at the Devil at all. He was looking at you, and I looked back at him.

Then I closed my eyes up tight and rubbed my temples again.

Oh Lord, fuck, shit, St Michael, sorry, I said to myself. *I don't really know why I'm doing this but I just should. I just want to say sorry for my sins in case I get some kind of punishment for it all. But I don't really know how to do it properly. I don't know any proper prayers. I mean, I knew them once, I believed in them then, but I just can't remember the exact words now. I hope you can understand whatever I try to say. Stuff that mightn't exactly be prayers. I hope to God you can understand English.*

This was no good. I was totally useless at this. I'm just no good at this shit; talking about shit.

I looked down at the tablets and steroids and shit again. Look, I said to myself. Get your head together. You've got to get your head together and say something. Now of all times.

Someone else knelt down on the bench beside me. Some woman who wasn't that old. She didn't look like a religious person, like some Holy Mary you might point out on the street. *Fuck it, look. Concentrate, Jerome. Get back to business.*

So I hope you can understand that I mean stuff but I can't say it properly. I can't say it in the way you'd probably want.

This woman was crying too. There were these little tears just overspilling and rolling down her cheeks a bit. There wasn't a big torrent or anything. She wasn't hysterical. She wasn't making sucking sounds in her throat. She just seemed sad in a gentle remembrance way like it was an anniversary or something. She blessed herself and got up and walked out of the church and I watched her as her heels clonked on the stone and she got to the door and left. Then I tried to make eye contact with the statue again.

See, I don't know, but I bet if I'd had a Ma then I'd be more of an all-right person. I'd be balanced and a good human being. I'd understand things about feelings more. Things wouldn't build up in me and come out in funny ways. I'd be better with Gary and

I could just put my hand on him or around him and we'd be like
mates like we were when shit shit shit shit shit shit shit shit shit,
I can't fucking do all this faggotty confessing-things shit.

Without hardly even realizing it I was back on my feet
again. I'd got up with my eyes closed and my knuckles still
rubbing my temples. There were a couple of echoes and
whooshes as the doors of the church opened and people came
inside and the traffic noise was sucked in and a bus passed by
and the doors closed again. There must have been some mass
starting soon. There weren't many people, but there were a few
religious types booking their seats early.

I needed to pretend I was doing something because I felt a
bit funny standing around like this. I walked back down the
aisle again and towards this basin in the wall where they kept
holy water. I bent my head down and cupped some water in
my hands and wetted my face. It was kind of reviving
although it smelled and tasted of pine like everything else in
the church, like they'd soaked the benches in it. I settled there
for a second, resting on the lip of the basin with my hand, and
just kind of got lost in the water with my eyes.

'Y'all right there, son?'

I thought I recognized the voice for a second and I didn't
want to look around because I wasn't right to talk to anyone.
I hadn't talked to anyone all day and the back of my mouth
was still all sealed up from the morning.

'You're not gonna be sick are you? You should go outside for
a bit.'

I had to say something now. 'No I'm grand, Mr Cowap,' I
mumbled with my back still turned.

'You what, sorry?'

'I'm grand, Mr Cowap,' I said as I turned around. 'I was just having a bit . . . come in here for some prayers, like.'

'Ah Jerome! How are you? Come in for a quiet word?'

'A bit. Sort of.'

'Well that's good to see. Are you hanging about for eight o'clock mass then?'

'Nah, I'm just finishing up like.'

'Right.' He looked around for a second like he was searching for a mate or something, so I said, 'See you', and made for the door. Then he followed me into the porch to get a leaflet.

'United are going well this season.'

I had to think for a second. 'Yeah. They're looking good all right.'

'Have to watch Arsenal though. I tell you, they've some team this season, Arsenal. They'll need watching.'

And then me and Mr Cowap had this chat about United, about the difference between this season and last season, and how it was a bit shit about the Champion's League and how Schmeichel wasn't the same keeper he was last year and how Phil Neville was shit and Keane was deadly, and I kind of got into it. And then some bloke that Mr Cowap knew came in the door and he got distracted for a while as he talked to him. I didn't know what to be doing for a minute so I went off. And it was only when I was back about half-way up through the green that I remembered leaving the medicines in the church, and hoped some kid wouldn't think they were sweets or something.

But I was grand now otherwise.

I know Gary heard me. He didn't make a noise but I know he must have heard me come in the back. I had the spare key for

the back door so I went round that way. Luckily he wasn't in
the kitchen. I was nearly ready to say something to him but
not quite yet. I'd need to brace myself a bit more. I figured he
was probably in the TV room, although there wasn't any
sound coming from the TV. Or maybe he was in his room. I
wasn't going to check. I walked upstairs as quietly as I could
and went into my own room.

I propped up a chair by the window and lit a fag. For some
reason I felt like opening the window to let the smoke out. It
wasn't like there'd ever been any restrictions or rules about
smoking in the house with Da; he smoked so much that he
could hardly have complained about me not opening a window.
I was just a bit more aware about it being stuffy right at that
moment and I wanted the room to breathe. It was also because
I felt all strange and guilty about smoking suddenly and I
thought to myself I wish Da had put the boot in when he caught
me with the smokes for the first time when I was thirteen.

I wondered why I found it hard to see out the window. I
realized like a daw then that my spotlight was on and I couldn't
see beyond the light inside the room reflected on the glass.
So I turned off the spotlight and sat in darkness and looked
out the window over the walls and fences. Then I decided
that this wasn't what I wanted. I felt a bit freaked sitting there
in the blackness. I turned the spotlight back on and looked at
my own reflection on the inside of the glass. It was good
because you could see yourself, but with the glare behind and
the darkness on the other side you couldn't make out too
much detail on the face. After a while I got ready for bed. I sat
up on the pillow, turned the spotlight over me and went
through a pile of old *Warlord* annuals I kept under my bed. I

read almost every story, and when I got tired I propped one of the annuals over my face for the smell, and I felt condensation wetness and I got sleepy.

I jumped out of bed. I thought I heard a noise outside on the landing. It was a sudden, knee-jerk thing. I was there with my eyes not really closed, but not seeing anything at the same time, and next thing there was a creak and I panicked and gulped in a breath and I was on my hands and knees on the floor. I knelt there waiting for my heart to slow down and to hear the noise again, but there was only silence. I wasn't sure for a second whether I'd imagined it or whether I'd stopped it in its tracks with the noise I made myself. Then there was this little *boo hoo, boo hoo, boo hoo woo.* Sniffling and *boo hoo.* It wasn't like he was trying to hide it. Just *boo hoo, boo hoo,* oh *boo hoo.* As if he wanted me to hear it. Ridiculous.

He was sitting on the top step of the stairs. There wasn't much light except for what was coming up from the porch, but I could see Gary's shape shaking with the whimpering and then stopping and then shaking again. He turned his face up at me. His cheeks and the skin above his lip were sparkling and the red had swollen up around his eye. His actual eyes weren't angry though. It was like they were looking for the right words to say, either out of his mouth or my mouth.

'What's been happening . . . I've . . . Jesus . . .'

I felt like saying, 'Toughen up faggot!' right at that moment. I wanted to light up a fag and say something to toughen up the situation. How dare he put me in this situation. I'd forgotten what I wanted to say to him earlier on. Making me feel like a weak fag like this.

'Toughen up faggot!'

I went back to bed and I thought I could hear him whimpering some more.

It was the first morning after my suspension from school. Gary was going to leave earlier than me to beat the traffic. After he had his last cup of tea, after he got his coat from the stairs and after he picked up his keys, he did this one last thing before he left the house. He ran up the stairs and came back down with this shoe box in his hands. His coat collar was up like he was about to jet off.

'Here. I found this in Da's wardrobe when I was clearing out the room. You should maybe have a look at it.'

I was glad he left giving me this box till just before he was going. I was glad he turned his back immediately and headed out for the car and didn't see the shock on my face. Even though I'd no idea what was inside the box I knew it was going to be a shock. It was the combination of secrecy, it being this box and it being hidden, and the mention of Da, and the mention that I should look at it. I didn't even have that initial feeling of surprise or curiosity. It was a feeling of shock immediately; I just knew it was going to be some big shit, like some new stage to tackle or enter. Gary might as well have left a bomb on the table.

I was looking for ways to delay opening that box. I was looking for a way not to have to look in it at all. I ate my breakfast very slowly. I messed with the knife on the bread. But I knew there was nothing much else between me finishing my breakfast and me having to leave for school. Everything else was ready for me to go. I was in one of those Catch-22s:

if I was to leave opening the box, then I knew I'd act all weird in school, thinking about it; if I opened the box, then I wasn't sure I'd be able to cope with school that day.

It was an awkward situation Gary dropped me in all right. I didn't blame him for it though. I blamed Da. He shouldn't have been hoarding all these secrets. Fuck it; I was probably making it into a big deal . . .

It was some old battered ancient thing, Dubarry or something. The corners were furry with wear and age. I found nothing particularly amazing to begin with inside; just these bits and bobs, these life-saving badges and old photos and shit. But up near the top was this batch of white envelopes. The one at the head of the pile was turned upside down. I turned it around and saw it was addressed to this house. All the envelopes had our address on them. They'd been opened already, like probably by Da years ago and then Gary whenever recently, but the flaps had been tucked closed again.

The other thing I noticed about the envelopes was that they had English stamps on them, Christmas stamps, and everyone was a different year, stretching back years and years. They were sort of bulging as well, as if whatever was put into the envelopes was slightly too big for them. Some of them had burst at the edges with the pressure and were showing different-colour paper inside: reds and blues. I lifted open the flap of one of them and found this other envelope inside. The one inside, all the ones inside, were totally sealed, like they'd never been opened before. You could see the dried paste of spit and gum overlap the level down the envelope a bit where the flap was closed over.

I hadn't recognized the handwriting with our address, but

this handwriting with this 'Hitchin & Bryant' address was definitely Da's. Most of the inside envelopes were addressed to this woman's name called Patricia in this house or place called 'Hitchin & Bryant' which was on this street in London, except for one or two earlier ones which were made out to Patricia in 'Wheeler Consulting' in London.

And then the card inside when I opened the envelope had this simple message on it, this message of 'Happy Christmas Patricia. Best wishes from Bobby, Jerome and Gary.'

And all the cards when I ripped open the envelopes had these simple messages inside them with 'Happy Christmas' and shit, and Da's name and my name before Gary's which was weird because Gary usually went first because he was the oldest. They all had the same shit inside them except for the first one or two from the Wheeler Consulting envelopes which had 'Baby Jerome' on them instead.

And then I put the cards back in the coloured envelopes and the coloured envelopes back in the white envelopes and the white envelopes back in the box and I didn't think for a good few minutes. Then I thought: no, I really *have* to go back to school because Nagle and Powell would go mad totally. And then I thought: no, I won't go to school. Fuck it, I'm going to do this. I'm going to do this and I can't believe I am. I'm going to go to London instead.

5

TWELVE

It was going through my head all the way to London on the plane, over and over again, even more than the actual significance of what I was doing, or the planning of what I was going to be doing, or the anxiety of what I was going to be doing: *I can't believe I'm making this happen; I can't believe I'm taking the reins here and sorting this out; for the first time in my life I'm doing something like this.* It must have been just the initial excitement.

I got a lucky break with the tickets. I just rang up and they said they had a cancellation for the following Monday, so that was that then. They were dirt cheap as well, except that the plane only left you at Stansted Airport, which was about 30 or 40 miles outside London, but it was only another fourteen quid for a train down, so it was grand really. No, all that was grand, the tickets and the money and shit; I was never really worried about it. It was only getting around Gary that might have been a problem.

I let on there was another retreat yokey. I thought a retreat would be kind of believable because I'd only be gone for two and a half days anyway. The ticket was from Monday morning till Wednesday morning, and that would be the sort of time you might spend on a retreat. I said that the trip down to

Powell's place down in Wexford that time had to be cancelled because part of the roof caved in on the castle.

'You never told me that at the time,' said Gary.

'I didn't think it mattered,' I said. 'I'd made my mind up when it happened that I wouldn't be going anyway, so I thought, "What was the point?"'

'So where's this new retreat?' I couldn't tell whether he was suspicious or not.

'It's some monastery place up in Cavan.'

'Cavan? Hm. And why've you decided to go on *this* retreat and not the last one?'

'I don't know. This just seems better. It's to get us in tune for our mocks and shit.'

He thought he'd play it cool then, stop being the concerned parent. 'Take whatever you need from expenses, so,' he said, pointing towards the old radio. I took out two twenty pound notes.

'Will that be enough?' he goes then.

'Ah yeah. Should be.'

I saw there was about another hundred quid in there when I was taking the money out. I said to myself that I must take the rest at the very last minute just before I leave for the airport. It turned out actually there was 125 quid. Together with that and the fifty-eight quid I had left in my bank account, I thought I might have enough.

The other thing then was the place I'd be staying. There was this *London A to Z* map book we had in the magazine stand in the TV room. It was one of the first things I remembered to pack as I was getting a few things ready on the Friday night. This business card dropped out as I was flicking through it. It had the name of a guest house near the centre of London that I remember me and Da and Gary stayed in the only other time I went to London when I was about seven or eight. It was bookmarking the page where the guesthouse was; it must have been there all these years. It was handy because the address was on the card and it was easy to find on the map.

Pretty soon after take-off I'd been thinking of how I'd pin my thoughts down in some way and of sending off a letter to the Farrellys when I got to London. Who else would I send the letter to? They were the ones I needed to explain most to. I'd never ever thought of carrying paper and pens around with me before, but while I'd been waiting around in the airport, I bought this biro and pad to write this letter on the plane. But it was difficult, I don't know. The ideas and some of the words were in my head, but it was impossible to get them down on paper in a way I wanted. It was difficult, and I bit my pen so hard that the plastic broke and caught a bit of my tongue between two splints and made it bleed. I was getting so frustrated with it I thought I'd get thrombosis in my leg. In the end I just crumpled the page up and put it on my breakfast tray for the gay air host to collect. I made sure that I'd scribbled over it really thick so the pilots and the cabin crew wouldn't have a laugh with it. Then I got worried for a second that I hadn't ripped it up into tiny bits.

This guesthouse I'd been planning on staying in was near Baker Street, where Sherlock Holmes was from. It was kind of a posh area, but the business card said it was as low a price as you could get for such a central location. It was so handy to get to, like everywhere in London. After the half-hour train ride from Stansted to Liverpool Street station, you got the tube seven stops up to Baker Street on the Circle Line and then you took a ten-minute walk and you were there. When I was on the tube I could remember clearly what Da said about how handy and efficient the transport was in London, about how everything was a rush, and you had to watch yourself getting on and off the train, but everything was pretty cheap and all the people who worked on the tube, or the bus or taxi drivers, the people on the services he called them, were really decent. And he's right; no matter what you say about the Brits, the people on the services are good folk, the blacks and that.

The guesthouse was like this normal house right in the middle of London; normal like a normal house you'd see on TV, not like an estate house from the sixties or whatever, but normal-redbricked normal. It was just in off the street and there was an empty canary cage and wind chimes in the porch and the woman seemed nice. She told me to hang on for a second while she looked after a few people who were settling with her at the counter, so I waited in the hallway.

And it was weird then because this really clear memory I had then had a shape to it. I was standing in the corridor looking into a room that I remembered so well from that other time I was in London. It was the way the room was shaped and laid out I remembered so well, with the bay window and the bumps on the ceiling, and the wallpaper was still the same, that sort of red furry paper like they had in The Tankard. The woman working there was different from the woman all those years ago though. It was the woman I remembered the best. She was Irish like us. Da had asked her to mind us for the day because he was going out on his own for a few hours. 'Why can't we go with you?' I remember Gary going. Yeah Da, why can't we go with you, I remember thinking. He'd been bringing us all over, to the wax museum, and this ship, and to White Hart Lane to see Spurs who I supported back then with Chris Waddle playing. He didn't answer Gary back. He just looked at the woman and winked at her.

'Thanks a lot, Jesus. You're great for doing this. I don't know how long I'll be but . . . y'know.' And he kind of winked at her again.

'Not at all. They'll be fine here with Mrs Moore . . .'

That was her name, Mrs Moore. She kept talking about herself as if she was someone else.

'. . . because Mrs Moore used to have children this age once, and Mrs Moore knows how to keep them out of trouble.'

And then she plonked us in the room and sat with us for a while, not really saying anything, just asking the usual questions. Then she brought down this Sesame Street colouring book and a kids' encyclopaedia with pictures of Romans. Gary was getting to that age where he didn't want to be doing shit like that. He was just hooshing himself up and down on the radiator with his hands all day looking out the window. I was kind of delighted though, for a while, sitting there with markers and the pictures which made you think of going back in time to Rome. But it was just the way Gary was moving around at the window. The woman had made me distracted for a few minutes, but then I got thinking again about why Da might have gone off for the day and left us behind. Gary was acting the most bored, but it was me who asked the woman first where Da had gone. She could see we were getting pissed off at this stage and Gary was too old for colouring books and shit, so she went off and got a video somewhere. This was way before we had a video in our house so we thought this was great. It was this rip-off of *ET*, but it kept us entertained. It only lasted about an hour and a bit though, and soon after we were back to being bored and sort of fidgety again. It had started to rain outside, and the woman left us to look after something or other at this stage. She'd forgotten to turn the lights on in the room and I remember just sitting there in the dimness with me and Gary silent, I think, although maybe I was whining, going, 'I'm bored, I'm bored.' Gary didn't know how to put the lights on because it was like a dial and every time he tried to turn it, it came off. We couldn't even watch TV because it was stuck on the video channel with the video over and the snowstorm going and we didn't know how to turn it over.

It was really late when Da came home. Me and Gary had moved into the hall to get some light and the woman found us there. She brought us into the kitchen and gave us Penguin bars. The door pushed open outside in the hall and it rang this bell. We rushed out for the hundredth time that day and this time it was Da.

'How'ya lads.'

He didn't say anything for ages then. He was really silent and his face was all . . . fucking . . . kind of . . .

Jesus, I remember. It was like someone had whupped his arse at snooker ten times in a row.

It was really embarrassing because the woman said they were all booked out. She thought I'd been waiting just to make enquiries, but when I said I was looking for a room immediately she could only say, 'Sorry', and point to this sign that said 'NO VACANCIES'. It would have been too steep anyhow. It was meant to be budget accommodation but it would have left things tight for the next two and a bit days if somehow there had been a room available and I had splashed out. She said there were cheaper rooms in town if I rang around. 'Here,' she said and she gave me a brochure. She said I could use the phone in the hall if I liked and she sold me a phone card.

I found this place – a hotel, not a guesthouse – eventually, down the Jubilee Line and then two stops up the Central Line in another area. It was funny because it was an even posher area, but the hotel was so much cheaper and tackier than the guesthouse. All the buildings around were brilliant white and they made you feel hot. It was as if they were collecting all the heat around and throwing it back down on the streets. The people who ran the hotel were foreigners, like Spanish or Italian, I couldn't make out. They had this weird flag I'd never seen before behind reception. I started pointing at it making small talk when I was checking in. I was feeling good about myself because I was doing things and getting things done.

'Where's that, like, one of the new countries? Is that where you're from?'

'Yes, it's where we're from,' the man sort of laughed, being polite. 'But it's not a new country. It's one of the oldest of all the countries.'

'Where is it? In Israel or somewhere?'

'No, it's the Basque country.'

'Oh yeah. I think I've heard of it.'

'Most people have heard of it, but not many know anything about it.'

'What are you, like Italians or something?'

'No. We're not like any other people in the world. Some of us say we were dropped in from another planet.'

'Sounds pretty deadly.'

'You're Irish?' he goes. 'I know a lot of Irish. I love Irish. We, all of us, the Basque people, love Irish. You're fighters . . .'

And then he starts trying to say something beginning with 'and', but I was butting in trying to say something not very funny about the 'fighters' bit. It was really embarrassing; every time he was going 'and' I started going 'It depends on what . . .', and then I'd stop, and he'd go 'and' again, and I'd speak over him again, going 'It depends on what . . .'. And then I stopped and he goes, 'And we like your beer.' I kind of made this stupid laugh then, and I went up to my room feeling shit. It was like one of those things that you can't explain when you make a fool of yourself talking and you just want to kill yourself like it's a feeling taking over for a moment.

It seemed like a whole day had gone because I'd done a lot and travelled so much, but it was still barely past lunchtime. The room in the hotel was all right for how cheap it was; small, like, but you could feel as if no one could get at you in it. It was right up the top under a slanty roof with a skylight you could swing up and stick your head out of. I wasn't sure if I was allowed smoke in the room. The guy at the desk might have said something about it but I didn't hear. I stood on the bed just in case and leaned out on the roof and had my first fag of the day. It was kind of a deadly view at first because of the tall buildings and the whiteness, but after a minute it got boring because you couldn't see over the first rim of buildings that surrounded you. There was this funny sound as well, this hum all around of cars in the distance and nearby. I'd never heard it so loud before, or so deep, like a million cars thick.

The easiest thing would have been to stay in the room, lying on the bed or looking out the window smoking. It was only now while I was hanging around doing nothing that the tiredness of the morning was creeping up. With all the rushing I'd forget for a bit what I was here for. At the start of the morning, getting up and the plane, I was excited and my mind was buzzing with what was ahead, even while I was letting on to Gary about the retreat or getting the plane tickets over the counter. Now though, here, my mind would go totally for maybe five minutes at a time, and when I would think at why I was here I'd kind of get worried.

Looking at the map, I could have walked up by the top of Hyde Park to get in towards the Oxford Street area, but I decided to get the Central Line back in instead. I headed out, leaving my stuff in the room, except for my money, because I was a bit worried about the other people in the hotel, and I went down to Lancaster Gate station. It was only a short walk, but you'd still get held up with all the people at the entrance. Then I got my ticket which I'd bought for the day at Liverpool Street, and stuck it in the slot and *shup* had it sucked out of my hand and *shup* collected it again out the other slot when the bar went over and went to where the train was going east. I went right for the centre of the crowd who were getting off, not giving them time to clear out of the way, and I had to turn my shoulders and go sideways a bit to stop bumping into people. The seats were pretty much all taken in the carriage I got on so I held on to one of the straps hanging down. Then you could hear the electricity, and the train started up and went on to Marble Arch where the woman with the posh voice went, 'Marble Arch' over the speaker, and then on to Bond Street, and the same. And then along the line between Bond Street and Oxford Circus one of the bulbs in the carriage started to go. It was flicking on and off really fast, and if you concentrated on it, it was going in time with the clack of the track. I closed my eyes to listen to the rhythm, and then opened them to see if the light had fallen out of step. Then I did it again and forgot about the sound and noticed the way the flicking came through my eyelids and wondered was this how people caught epilepsy and said Mam, Mam, Mam to myself, actually whispering it, not Ma, Ma, Ma, like I'd been calling my Ma in my head, but Mam, Mam, Mam, because I liked the way the word ended in *mmm* because it was sort of nice, whispering it again and again and over again. And I suddenly noticed the posh voice again, going 'Oxford Circus', but it was like a delayed reaction, like she'd said it a while back and it had been swirling around in my ear for ages but had only registered now. I took in a gulp of air and opened my eyes and just as I did, just barely having heard the words 'Oxford Circus', the voice said 'Tottenham Court Road' as the train stopped again.

'Fuck it! Fuck it!'

I pushed myself through the people getting off and ran up the platform looking for an exit. Then I came out under this massive slab stretching way up and I could see Oxford Street up before me. I started to jog up the street to get to Oxford Circus, which was about half-way up the street. I needed to get to Oxford Circus because I had it all worked out from there.

When I reached the entrance of Oxford Circus, I turned

back a bit towards the way I came, and I crossed the road and went up a street. I was sprinting by this stage. Then I turned off onto another street and started to slow down, because I knew this was the street. I counted the numbers: twenty-four and twenty-two and twenty and eighteen and here I was at this Hitchin & Bryant place. A small brass plaque on a wall beside a door.

I waited for a minute to compose myself and to give time for the clamminess to go and my heart to slow down. I noticed someone coming up the street. I didn't want to look odd standing there on my own with my hand on the railing on a street where there were no shops or anything, so I pushed the door of Hitchin & Bryant open.

I came into this reception area. There was a desk on the right and a set of glass doors with a stairs behind it in front of me. The desk was empty. I was about to make for the stairs, kind of walking slowly and cautiously, when I heard a creaking from behind the desk, like someone had come out from another door in behind, and then a voice went, 'Sorry can I help you?'

I looked around and there was this woman there, about forty.

'I'm just looking for someone,' I said.

'Who are you looking for? I'll buzz them,' said the woman.

I thought for a second. 'My Ma. My mother.'

'Who's your mother?'

'Patricia.'

The woman looked sort of cross or confused. 'Well then you should know that Patricia is on maternity leave at the moment.'

'What, like, she's having a baby?'

'Had one. Just the other week. Shouldn't you know all this if you're her son?'

I went blank for a second. I couldn't think of anything to say. I couldn't look at the woman.

'No. I shouldn't know it. I wouldn't know it.'

I felt funny. The woman looked all awkward.

'Are you okay? Are you upset? I don't . . .'

I couldn't keep it in. I was welling up and I could feel a stone in my throat and then I just blubbed.

'Hey now. Hey now.' She came out from behind the counter. 'I don't know what to do for you, son. If you were expecting to see her here she's not around. You'll have to go out to the house.'

I wanted to ask where the house was, but that would have sounded suspicious. I didn't want to sound like a stranger. I didn't know what to do. I was hoping she'd just *say* the address. I didn't know what to do or say. I felt really uneasy and I could sense that she did too. I just didn't know what to say now, but I couldn't let it all collapse at this point. I cried some more.

'What's going on?'

I cried on and on, not bawling or anything, just sort of weeping, and I heard this man's voice: 'What's going on? Is everything all right, Laurie? Can we help you, son?'

'Tom, this is Patricia's son.'

'Her son? Grown up fast, hasn't he?' the man said to the woman. 'What's your name?' he asked me.

'Jerome.'

'Jermaine?'

'Jerome. Jerome Morris. I'm her son from Ireland.'

'Morris. From Ireland. Okay, son. You've travelled a bit?'

'Came here today. I'm lost. I got upset. I don't know why. I'm sorry.'

I looked up. I'd been leaning against the wall beside the desk. The man and the woman were standing there, and the man had his hand on my shoulder, squeezing it. Both of them looked kind. They looked like they understood me. The man was sort of pushing his bottom lip into his top lip and making his chin go dimply.

'Your mum's not here right now, you know that?' said the man.

'I know. The lady told me. I just thought she might have come back. I thought you could go back to work after a week when you had a baby. I just . . .' I thought hard, '. . . I'm going to go out to the house later on anyway.'

'So you've not come here to rob us or to shoot us all dead then?' asked the man.

'No! No way! No. I was just . . .'

The two of them started laughing.

'Come on, son. Come up with me. You could do us a favour if you're going out there.' The man was heading for the doors to the stairs. 'We've had a fair bit of mail for Patricia this last week. Some people probably think she lives in the bloody place. Used to spend most of her time here, building it up. It's really her home from home. Maybe this kid will give her some new priorities.'

We came to the top of the stairs and into an office.

'She told us to open any letters sent to her; any business stuff, we'd just look after, any personal, we send out to the house. Package arrived here this morning. Where'd I put it? Just put it into a new envelope before I popped out there.' He pointed to a ripped-up envelope lying at the top of an over-flowing bin, as he was looking around. 'Where is it?'

I picked up the envelope the package was sent in. It had the name 'Patricia Bryant' on the top.

'Bryant,' I said to myself out loud. 'It doesn't suit her.'

'Whoa, you're lucky George's not around to knock your head off. Used to be a handy enough fighter in his day. Georgie Bryant, pride of Penge. Before he turned his hand to psychiatric nursing.'

'Patricia Bryant. So my Ma's your boss then. Is she a good boss?' I asked.

'I'm telling you, your Mum built this place up almost sin-glehandedly. Bob had the . . .'

'Bob?'

'Bob. Yeah. Bob Hitchin. He had the connections, but your mum had the real talent. Won us "Most Promising Small Public Relations Firm" at last year's industry do, did your mum. That's who I'd put it down to. Very talented woman. She's a hard grafter too, though. Served a tough enough apprenticeship at Wheeler's – the bastards!'

'Do you know my Ma well?'

'I can't say I do, no. I'm only here about six months. But even from what I've seen so far, I can tell that your mother is . . . oh, here it is!'

He handed me the package. The big envelope was blank except for an 'If undelivered, please return to . . .' note at the top.

'You didn't put my Ma's address on it,' I said.

'No, I didn't get around to it,' the man said. 'But, you know, you're going around so . . .' He paused for a second. 'You do know where to go, don't you?'

'Yes, I do.' *Yes, I do*. I didn't know why I'd said that. If I'd said 'No', because I was her son from Ireland who she hadn't seen since I was ten – and I'd have only been half lying and it probably would have been something along the lines of what he'd been assuming anyway – and she'd invited me over but I'd lost her address, he would have just given me the address. But I said, 'Yes, I do', and it made things more complicated.

'Good then. Well have a good day son.'

I went back down with the man to the reception area. The woman behind the desk smiled as I passed by. 'Wish your mum well from me. Laurie's my name. You look very like her, you know.'

'He does actually,' said the man. 'Very like her.'

'Really?' I went.

'Yes you do,' said the man.

'He does. Very like her.'

'People say that all right.'

'You do look like her,' said the man again.

I was left on the street with this bundle and I hadn't any idea what to do with it. I had nothing left to do in London. I turned the corner back towards Oxford Street. There was a load of people and I just went with it.

All these things, these shops, and all these folks running around, and the buzz, and nothing left to do.

I was getting hungry so I stopped in this steak-house place and had a hamburger and chips and a sponge and two cokes, and then a Carlsberg. There was this thick science fiction comic book that someone had left behind about a green woman that I looked at. Then I wandered around Oxford Street for ages. I went into this place, the Trocadero, for a while and browsed through the video section of a CD shop in there. They were giving away posters free from this pile, and I found a deadly one of *Cliffhanger* that I was going to take, but then I thought it might be too awkward to carry around with this bundle I had as well, and I thought it might get crumpled and creased, so I left it. After that I went across the road and up a bit to another CD shop. They had these deadly books in this section. One of them told you how to lift up a lock in a car.

I went on down Oxford Street in the direction I walked from Tottenham Court Road station, towards the huge building I saw when I came up into the street that time. The sign at the top was flicking on in the dark and it said 'CENTRE POINT'. I turned off to the right before I came to it. There was these neon signs down the end of the street, really pink and eighties. This Indian guy scared the shit out of me as I went by. He was standing outside of this restaurant with a funny tall hat going 'Would you like a taste of Nepal, sir? Would you like a taste of Nepal, sir?' The signs all belonged to strip joints, and here and there were shops selling porn and dirty videos and masks with zips across the face and shit. I found it kind of disgusting.

I wound through the streets around Soho and then came out on Charing Cross Road. It had all these bookshops, loads and loads of bookshops, all the same. I kept going along until I came to Trafalgar Square. It was quite dark and there weren't as many people around as you'd expect. Most of the people seemed to be foreign students in bright-coloured puffer jackets looking into books. There were still a few pigeons flying around, although maybe they were bats.

I went down one side of Trafalgar Square and down this street on the left where I could see the river stretching across ahead. There's something about rivers in cities which I like. I've only seen one apart from the Thames — the Liffey in Dublin — but they're my favourite part of cities. You feel like you're smack in the middle of town when you walk by the river, like everything centres on it and is sliding into it. I like the way they never stop moving as well, like they've been doing for hundreds of years, with all bits of history that's fallen into them and trapped in mud — knights, vikings, old boats, bottles. And I like the way they move in one direction; always out to something else, like a world beyond. You get the same feeling thinking about it as when you look up and your eyes adjust and you notice more and more stars.

There's always stuff going on on the river in London. The Liffey's too narrow and the bridges too low, but with the Thames there are always boats going up and down, and boats moored on docks, police boats with flashing lights, and boats that make loud mechanical noises. It was great to just walk along and watch all the night-time traffic. It was like a different level of busy-ness to the rest of London. And there was this ream of lights hanging along by the banks, all goldie like bunting lit up, like Christmas lights they never take down on 7 January.

I kept going, past this Egyptian tomb, and along round this curve in the river, and I tried to keep as close to the wall at the bank as much as I could, until the road went in an underpass, under a bridge and away from the river. I wandered on down this street for ages, going under these road bridges. It seemed like I was getting further away from the river. Then I remembered that if I was going the way the river flowed I'd be heading east, and I knew that the East End was a dodgy area. But up further on was the Tower Bridge, all floodlit. I walked on towards it, and then I came to this big building to my right, nearer the river. I recognized it straight away, those onion towers; it was the Tower of London, where they'd tried to rob the crown jewels.

Up on the left was the sign for Tower Hill tube station. I was starting to get tired so I went up the steps towards the entrance to the station. Outside the door this crowd of people had gathered. They were turned towards this woman with scraggly hair. She was going on like, 'Is everyone ready, are we ready to start the Jack the Ripper tour?' I stopped when I heard that. I'd heard about it before, Jack the Ripper, and I was into shit like that. I wondered if I'd be able to tag along at the back and not have the woman notice.

The tour took a route up into this part of town with modern buildings. We came into a square surrounded by sky-scrapers and the woman said that this was where Jack the Ripper murdered someone. I found it hard to believe until I looked down and saw the square was paved with old cobble-stones. The woman saw me scanning the ground and said, 'Yes, just about on that spot there; can you feel it sticky under-foot?' We made a turn beyond this wall that the woman said the Romans built and was now the dividing line between the East End and some other part. The buildings were totally dif-ferent on the other side of the wall. They were older and lower and shabbier. We went around through all these alleys in crap light, and every so often some Pakistani would lean out of a window and shout at us. The woman told us not to mind, and we carried on going to all these places where Jack the Ripper had cut women up.

After about two hours, we wound up in an old pub that the woman said Jack the Ripper would have drank in. I got the feeling she was looking here to get money off people who couldn't find the right change at the start, so I left the group and headed back the way we came from the modern part of the city.

If I'd thought about it too much, the walk back would have put the shits up me, but I wasn't even thinking of the danger and the darkness. If I'd thought too much about some of the shit the tour-guide woman was telling us I would have been a wreck. But it didn't really bother me. I noticed these blocks of flats that I hadn't seen on the way out, stretching way up all brown against the black. It was a really dodgy place, but it never occurred to me that some of the Pakistanis that had been shouting at us could have come down for me with a machete or a knife or some shit. I just kept on walking because my mind was buzzing while I was on my own.

The streets on the other side of the old wall were as deserted. All the people who worked in the skyscrapers had gone home or had gone to pubs and clubs in other areas. It was even lonelier here. At least in the other part you knew there were people asleep or watching TV behind the windows.

When I got to this one area I could hear this low bass thud coming from somewhere. It was hard to work out; it was either from really far away and I'd just come within earshot, or

it was indoors somewhere quite near. I walked towards this
corner and the sound seemed to get louder. It was still low and
muffled, but it was definitely getting louder with each foot-
step. When I turned the corner, I saw that the ground floor of
one of the buildings was glazed from top to bottom like a fish
tank. There were people moving around inside in dim light.
Some were sitting down on big soft chairs and couches and
some were leaning at a bar. All the blokes had proper suits on;
lots of them had taken their ties off. Some of the women had
suits on as well, but most just had normal fancy clothes or
dresses or frocks.

I went up closer to hear this bass line. It was going *dvvv-
dvvv dv dv dv*, on and on. It was hard to tell the tune.
Something was swilling around in my head, but it was hard to
tell. There was a sort of a cage in there as well with a funny
monkey in it.

This hand comes in a blade into my groin and then cups up
and squeezes my arse.

'Wanker doorman's been acting tough again has he?'

I thought for a second I'd been got by a faggot. But before
I was able to turn around and look I got a smell of all spicy
perfume and then I felt this nice soft breath of mint and fags
on my cheek and the voice went again: 'Just hold tight.' And
she was actually *walking* me, pushing her hand where it was
positioned and making me move forward with her.

When we got to the door, she moved her hand up and
around my waist and we breezed by the guy at the door no
bother. I was probably dressed in the best clothes I had
anyway – beige slacks, and my wine sweatshirt and my old
school shirt, from my uniform before they banned them, on

underneath. Inside I got a better look at the woman. She had blonde hair in a tight helmet and a not-bad face until she smiled, and then you saw these crooked teeth and those gums where they went in behind the tops of the teeth. She was smiling and bobbing her head around quickly from side to side like a bit of a fool. She was smiling and laughing because she seemed to be saying, 'Look what I'm going to do', and then she went into the porch again and jabbed the bouncer sharp in the kidneys with her fingers. She was giggling and saying something to him and he half-smiled and half-looked over his shoulder all coolly like, 'Not fucking her again.' Then she came back in and her mouth was going yap yap yap to me but I couldn't hear a word because the music was so loud. She made this sort of 'never-mind' gesture, patting the air with her hand, and then she pointed to me and pointed to the ground and went off to the bar. When she came back wiggling her arse and hips and staring at me she had these two blue cocktails in cone glasses with umbrellas. She handed me one of the glasses and raised the other one to her mouth. She said something again but I still couldn't hear. I took a sip out of my glass and nearly died. It was like drinking something you'd stick in a machine to make it work. I started coughing and spluttering, with tears coming out of my nose and my eyes going all watery, but it was so loud in the bar you wouldn't notice the noises I was making. It was the kind of place where if you farted it would be too loud to hear it and there'd be too many different smells to smell it.

There was sort of movement near us as this group got up from seats around a glass table. I sat into one of the seats and put the drink and the envelope on the table. When I looked up the girl was staring at me and laughing. She took a grip of the shoulder of my sweatshirt and started to pull me but I kind of froze in confusion for a second like, 'Where are you bringing me?', and I wouldn't budge, like my tensing up made me two times my weight. Then she started to back away, all the time still staring at me, and she made this sexy 'come here' move with her finger. Her eyes seemed to stay fixed on me even as she was turning around. I looked around to see was anyone else seeing this. She was still walking and she'd keep looking around to see if I was following. She seemed totally gone in the head. I got up from the seat and looked around again and followed her to the toilets.

There was one of those sort of anterooms where the door to the men's and women's toilets were. It was brighter, really bright, and much quieter than outside.

I suddenly wondered what the fuck I was doing in there.

I started to get a bit panicked and wondered why I'd allowed myself to be even led into the club. The girl was looking and smiling at me and her teeth were worse than they looked outside. Her make-up was on weird and you could see that underneath the foundation she had those porridgey freckles that make me think of milk in a bowl. I could hear her voice now and it was husky and cockney and it panicked me even more.

'I'm Sue, short for Susan.'

I could feel my face burning up all red even though it was cool in the anteroom.

'Well? What's your name?'

'Me? Jerome.'

'I'm . . . that name's nice because . . . Did someone tell tall tell you I'd be here because I'm always here don't mind me too much 'cos I'm pissed was on . . . was down at Uhuru the new place. That's a strange name. Isn't it Jamaican is it?'

'It's Irish.'

'O-o-o-o-h! My gran was paddy Irish. Paddy gran's her name though she's dead now. We didn't cremate her. Here . . .'

She literally made this lunge with her mouth open. Me there and my cheek and her breath and her teeth all at once.

I was out of there. I went into the men's first and pretended to go for a piss. I was standing there for a bit with no piss coming out and I could tell people were thinking I was strange standing there with no piss coming out with my mickey out twaddling it about there. Then I ran back into the anteroom and that Susan was still there, waiting, going, 'There he is, my Irish Molly!'

Even for the spring it was cold. You kind of associate London with cold and snow, even though it's usually hot with all the people and the electricity coming up from the underground. But there were no clouds and all the heat just went *vwoosh* up and out and escaped. I was looking at my breath and going, Mam, Mam again, exhaling the steam; Mam, Mam, Mam, and my breath was all icy. Then I found this tube station called Bank and went down and it was warm again.

The Basque bloke was sitting at the desk. He was sitting there with a big grin as I approached him. I could tell he wanted to start some stupid conversation. I just turned to the right at the desk immediately, and I made myself fall against the wall as I approached the stairs to make it look like I was drunk.

'Ay! The toilets have some problem tonight, sir. There is very little water,' he shouted up behind me.

In bed in the hotel that night I thought about that dream I had that time when I escaped from the castle and had to find my way home. It seems more appealing that way, escaping from somewhere and finding your way home. I thought about those guys in Beirut and how they must have thought of it and planned it, chained to radiators. The route through the maze of alleyways and the run down to the coast and the payment to some fisherman to bring them to somewhere safe, an island, and the idea driving them on. I thought, wouldn't it be deadly to do it now, to escape from the hotel in the middle of the night and go to my Ma's house; just go to the address, sneak past the Basque bloke and go there. I figured, I'd walk; there'd be no tube at this time, so I'd walk and keep going.

THIRTEEN

The envelope, Jesus, shit.

I don't know why I'm so thick sometimes. I'm so forgetful and so thick. Usually I'm all right but sometimes, I don't know. It's like, I got up late from the walking and the night before, and I went to this kiosk around the corner to get a breakfast roll because I'd missed breakfast in the hotel, because breakfast was eight o'clock to half ten or something, so I went to this kiosk to get breakfast. The dick in the place was going, 'Awoight, yah yah yah yah yah', on and on, driving me mad, 'mental, facking mental' as he was going, so I didn't go for one of the picnic benches with the builders and the porno calendars or the spoons lying around with the tea in them. I went over to this other place across the road, this pub, and as soon as the barman got the whiff of the eggs and rashers, and me sitting down not having ordered, he was, 'Customers only, son. Nowhere to go this time 'morning?' And I thought, 'No. I should, though. If only I had the address on that . . . shit!' Shit. The envelope, the envelope, the envelope. I'd forgotten the fucking envelope.

I'm conscientious that way. I don't like to fuck people around. Even if it's something that'll have no consequences for me, I don't like to have it playing on my mind knowing that someone will be put out of joint if it's anything I can help.

I was away over there like a shot, that bar near the Bank station, worrying as I was going over, shit is this place going to be open, shit what if it's nicked, shit could I be totally sure I left it there, shit will I find the place again?

I found it okay, even if it looked different in the daytime with the light coming off the glass instead of through it, but it was the size of the panes and the chrome you couldn't mistake. There were guys outside making deliveries from a truck and someone sweeping the path just outside the door.

'I wonder did you've, might you've, come across something last night I might have left in the bar,' I said to the guy doing the sweeping.

'Don't know nothing about it mate. Bernard inside's who you'd want to talk to.'

He was pointing inside so I assumed he was giving me the go ahead. I went in and there were guys cleaning.

'I'm wondering if you might have come across this envelope last night. Big thing. Brown,' I said to the first person I saw, making the shape with my hands.

'Oh yeah. Handed in last night. Big thing, yeah, with a return address in the West End?'

'Yeah. Did you send it back?'

'Eh. Don't think so. Not last time I looked. Hang on a minute.' He went up behind the bar. 'This it? Address in the West End.'

Luckily they had a post box at Hitchin & Bryant, to the side of the front door. I could shove the envelope in without having to go inside. It was soft and mushy and could be squeezed up to quarter of its size and I forced it into the gap.

And that was it, I was thinking. Hours to kill now, the whole day and the night, hours till the plane the next morning.

I wandered for a good bit around the streets with no shops, and then I noticed it was past the normal time when I took lunch and I was getting hungry. I walked round to Oxford Street and went to another one of those steak houses. I got a chicken thing and a bowl of chips, and I sat by the window.

I was watching this van move slowly in the traffic outside. It was just like a toy, like toytown. It was just like the van you'd see in Postman Pat, red and bright. A lot of London was like that, clean and basic and blocky and bright, all what you'd be used to seeing on kids' TV. I suppose you needed to come from the outside to look on it in that way, when you're just getting these images fed to you and they look right on the TV, but when you see them for real it looks comical, and it's the accents and shit as well, accents you'd only associate with the TV, and then the rhythm of the voices seems something weird. But these things are real for the people that live here, and everyday, and unnoticeable. I don't notice the post vans in Ireland. It was funny with the post, me not sending many things by post and not knowing the times, and I wondered would post vans be moving through the streets of Dublin at this exact time and then I wondered, shit, I was thinking, yeah shit, yeah, yeah, yeah . . .

'Hey! The bill!' some Chinese girl was going.

The door was off its latch again when I pushed it, even though I noticed a buzzer this time. That woman Laurie was there behind the desk. It took a second for her to remind herself who I was.

'Excuse me, sorry . . . Patricia's son?! Steady on, what's the rush?'

'Has the post come yet?'

'The post? What, you mean, has the post been delivered yet?'

'No, has it been collected yet.'

'No. It'll be around soon enough.'

'Where's Paul?'

'Paul?'

'Tom.'

'Just hang on a second.'

The woman buzzed Tom. 'He says go on up.'

'Aye, aye. Aye, aye,' goes Tom. 'What's the panic?'

'Look. I'm really sorry, I'm stupid . . . I was out and I left the fucking envelope down in this bar but I was there this morning and they said . . . well, so basically I came back because they said they'd sent it back up, with the address on it for here . . . and, well, I'm going back down now again, to the house, like, my Ma's house, so if they gave you back the envelope I'll save time . . .'

'Hey, hey. Relax. Here. Got it here.'

Tom handed me back the envelope. He'd written this new address in big, thick black marker.

FOURTEEN

I was lucky with the map. There weren't many lines on the Underground going into the south of London, but one of the few there was went near enough to Kingston. I had a job finding it at first on the map at the start of the *A to Z*, but there it was, way down on the left, below the river. The map on the back cover said the last stop on the District Line went to Wimbledon station. Kingston then was over below Wimbledon Common and Richmond Park. You could walk it. I asked someone about it. They said you could, you could walk it. They said you'd know the area because people had back gardens.

You'd notice it when you started walking from the station a bit of the way towards Kingston. They were like the houses out by Funderland. It was like the gardens and the houses were put up first and then the roads had to wind their way around these gardens that they built. It was awkward because there was no straight route to Kingston that way. You had to keep your wits about you. I thought I was okay though. I'd planned the route out on the *A to Z*. I had the tube ride to mark it out on the map with a biro and I put an 'X' where the house was. I kept having to look down at the map to make sure I was keeping on the line. I must have looked like a tourist, or a real obvious stranger, in this place. I was a bit worried I might get mugged. I strayed up the wrong end of a road somewhere and a ball nearly hit me from a golf course.

There was this shop I dropped into along the way. It was sunny and I was getting thirsty. This shop had a sign outside it saying they had teas and ices and sandwiches and pasties. I was only looking for a drink firstly, but when I saw that word 'pasties', it was one of those things that went 'yum', like a word where you can imagine the food. They had a small section in the back of the shop with wooden stools, and I got a bottle of Lucozade and a pasty. I didn't finish it. It wasn't anything like the word, all creamy; it was like a branch, or a fire-log, reheated in a microwave. When I got up to leave I noticed these flowers for sale in buckets. I bought a bouquet of these white and pink ones. The woman said they were carnations. After I'd left the shop and walked a couple of streets further towards Kingston, I noticed I'd left the envelope behind again. Fuck it though. I had these flowers now. They were only clothes for that baby in the envelope and I had these carnations to give over now.

I'd seen these streets before. They were just like the ones in one of the magazines Da had about the war. There were pictures in those magazines, all tinted up in blurry colours after being developed in black and white, of streets of houses that looked like these. I'd seen the same sort of houses later in a TV documentary. There used to be guys around here when the Germans were bombing London with helmets like the British soldiers, only painted black with ARP or ATP or something on them. They'd go around on bikes with hatchets. They'd go around these houses with women standing in the front gardens with flowery dresses smashing windows with hatchets rescuing people from blazes. It must be one of the most satis-fying things in the world that, smashing a window with a hatchet. A small one with a red-painted handle. Just taking it to the window and watching it fold in. Another thing I'd like to take a hatchet to would be one of those metal balls that hang up above petrol pumps in garages that tell you price and quantity. There'd just be something about swinging a hatchet or an axe into the metal of one of those things and watching a small explosion with sparks. In the attics of all these houses too they've stuff stored from the war: code machines, sand bags, unexploded bombs. It'd be great to break in and get one of those guns on a tripod with the six revolving barrels that take a day to cool down. You'd set it up on a bit of a bank and you'd point it and I'd say – I'd say to some of those who'd have been slagging me off for being into the war in school, bringing canteens and straps that Da had bought me in Blackrock market up to the teacher, and getting slagged off just because I wasn't into other shit – I'd point it and I'd go, 'Right fuck-face, get moving. On the count of ten. Ten, nine . . .' They'd go, 'Jerome, you're sound. We thought you were sound all along', and I'd be going, 'Too late. You say it now but, too late. Get your fucking arse moving. Eight, seven . . .' And the cunt would start zig-zagging, like something you'd learn out of the *SAS Survival Handbook*, running from side to side thinking he'll avoid the bullets that way. But then I'd hit nought, and I'd squeeze the trigger, and I'd let loose. And you'd light up the air with those things, you'd actually *see* the bullets like little fireflies. It's not like the films where they don't have special effects to streak the bullets across the screen; in real life the tracers would light up, you'd see the trajectories, the spray panning in this arc. But maybe the dick would wise up so as not to get mowed down and he'd dive into a shell crater. He'd hide under the muddy water until my rounds were used up. There'd be the sound of rapid fire and then this would stop, and the barrels would be whirring, and then this would slow to a metallic click-clack, with the smoke coming out like a fag. At that point I'd go over and I'd stand over and take out one of my rusty bayonets. And I'd stand there so he'd see me with it and watch him drown in the mud.

Eyot View. Number 24.

It was on the corner. The houses started on the other side of the road and went up and curled around a cul-de-sac and came back down and ended with 24. It seemed to have this big garden to itself. There was a front garden, a back garden, and there must have been a piece of land at the side which linked the two because the hedge wrapped right around.

There was a little grey car in the driveway. The driveway had sort of rough red tiles instead of tarmac. There was an oil patch in front of the car.

There were funny pillars in the porch painted white with grooves in them. They treated the porch like it was another room of the house – it was big enough to be one! There was this statue with its arms cut off. There were pots of flowers in it and one small barrel with this strange plant spilling out the top.

What was that thing I was to remember? Oh yeah; the comb in my back pocket. It had warmed up to arse temperature and gone soft and bent with my walking and I hadn't noticed it all day. I took it out and pulled it across my head. I made sure all the knots in my hair were ploughed out and I gave myself a side parting. I made my hair fall with the angle it grew out of my head. Then I ruffled the carnations and I rang the bell.

I waited about a minute and then I rang it again. Then I waited another minute and rang it again. It was like with Pot Noodles where you have to keep stirring and waiting.

The third time I rang it I put my ear up to the door. I was waiting for a sound, a door inside closing or a floor board or something. I pushed open the letter box. It was like an old antique thing; no stiff spring to keep it down, just a swing and a little screech.

Every house has its own distinctive smell. It's weird. Even from the letter box of our house, you can get this smell from inside of Dip Dabs, or Shake 'n' Vac, or something. With here it was like nature. It wasn't like a chemical thing. It was like a forest with trees. You could get a slint of the hall as well. In our house, you could see right up into the kitchen and out the back window if the kitchen door was open. Here you could see this nearly empty shelf with one object on it, a little sculpture. It was this thing that was meant to look like a hand twisted around. The bit of the floor I could see was all bare. There was no carpet or anything. It looked like she just got it and polished it.

She had this bay window at the front. It was coming out from the wall like a pipe. In our house it was hard to see in because of the net curtains, but here you could see right in if you cupped your hands around your eyes at the glass. There was this huge room going the full length of the house. It was like the bit of the hall, bare and icy and not very Christmassy you'd imagine. It had those wooden floor boards running into it, like they continued under the wall from the hall, and rugs, and tables of glass. There was this painting on the wall of real-life sand pouring out and spilling on to a pile of stuck-on sand on the floor, and little metal ants stuck going down like a joke. There was this other metal animal, like a shrimp made out of bits of metal, all welded, and rusted, and plonked in the middle of the floor for no reason. I looked for photographs on the shelves but I couldn't see any. I wondered if there were other windows that looked into other rooms.

She had a gate around the side with a handle and one of those pads for your thumbs. I pressed the pad and it went right down. She'd left it unlocked and I pushed it and went through.

The back wasn't as big as I expected from the size of the house. It was still about twice the size of the garden at home, but from the look of the house you'd expect this big stretch with the grass mowed to strips in different shades. It was just pretty normal, except there was a slide in bright colours. The slide was about as high as me. It had a ladder up the back with ten rungs in multi-colours too. There was this slide and a small paddling pool with no water in it.

I went up to one of the windows at the back. She had her TV room there. There was no clutter in it like our TV room at home. The only clutter was this play pen and a few toys thrown around. The toys looked like something for an older kid, all Action Men and plastic figures. There were no photographs in this room either. There were hardly any shelves to put them on. There was just this one with a few books and videos. She had this chest beside the TV as well. I wondered what was in it.

At first I thought, It's just out on the road. But then I heard it coming up the driveway, this car going *vooooo-o-o-om*, slower and slower to a halt, and then *bang*, these car doors shutting.

I ran for the hedge, straight into it, not thinking, just thinking it would give way. I went through the leaves and then into the sticks. It was all prickly and no light got through to the inside through the dark shiny leaves. It was really dense, and it was ripping and tearing at me, and my collar came off. The sticks were breaking, but only with the sheer force, and I was walking forward and forward and not thinking, and the twigs were sticking in my eyes and going up my nose. All the time I was holding on to the flowers but they were getting caught up and the petals were coming off. And I was driving, and it must have been only a few inches, but I had to keep on going, driving like a robot until I came to the wall at the other side. The wall only came up to my knees, but there were railings at the top that were hidden from both sides because the little dark leaves wrapped around them. I kind of swam up inside the hedge using my arms like flaps, but I had to let go of the flowers. I could wade upwards and the sticks kind of supported me, although they jabbed into my armpits. Then I grabbed hold of the railings and pulled myself over the spikes. They were blunted after hundreds of years of being banged but they still stuck in between my ribs like some kind of monster's teeth. I flopped on to the path on the other side, trying to break my fall with my arms. I lay there under the small height of the wall with my cuts all in this dog pee. I lay and I

listened some more because all I could hear in the hedge was
crshtsrcccshhshicshicshic.

There was nothing for a few minutes and then I heard a
rush of noise like when a bunch of people are talking all
together behind a door and there's a muffle and then the door
opens and the sound spreads out. Then there was the sound of
sort of a ball bouncing and a kid and a man and a woman and
names being repeated.

'Here, George!'

'Have to get it off me Trish!'

'Pass it Dad!'

'That's not fair!'

'Come on, Mum, tackle me!'

'Here, Cam, here . . . don't get tackled by a girl, you big
blouse!'

'See, see what I was saying?!'

'Back to me, Mum!'

'What is *that*?'

'What?'

'The hole in the hedge. Have we been burgled?'

It went all quiet, and then I could sense someone getting
nearer. Heavy breathing from stopping after running around,
and muttering. I hugged the wall tight. There was the sound
of rustling. Someone was at the rails above. I turned my head
really carefully up. There was a nose just peeping out from
between two rails, like the nose of a black man.

'What the fuck?' he was saying all quiet to himself, like he
was trying for the kid not to hear. 'What's with all these flowers?'

'What is it?' The woman's voice was up nearer now. It was

funny. It was kind of an English voice, but there was definitely that Irish 'T'. The way it just whistled and trailed off.

'Dunn . . . oof!' There was the noise of a ball being banged against someone's head and then smacking the hedge. 'Hey! Gotta cry foul on that!' went the man.

The ball bobbled off the top of the hedge and dropped on the ground with a bounce.

'Go get it Sparky!'

It went in decreasing little bounces off the path and on to the road.

'No, George. He's got to mind the road. I'll get it.'

It rolled back with the slope of the road and settled beside the kerb. It was a Manchester United ball. Like the one we had at home. Except this one had Eric Cantona instead of Kevin Moran on it. Just his face looking out all moody and his signature.

The gate on the side of the house clacked with the handle and then the front gate screeched.

It was hard picking myself up. Being in the one position like that and with the pain of the bushes. I got up and I was sort of stiff. I looked at the ball for a second and I thought . . . I don't know.

I picked up the ball.

I picked up the ball and I was going to throw it back and make it up from there.

'Hey! What are you doing?!'

It was definitely an Irish accent. You could hear it now. I didn't turn around.

'Give that back!'

There was a hardness to it though.

'Where are you going? Give that back!'

I walked on and turned the corner. I didn't look around.

'Were you the guy in our garden?!'

I flung the ball over my shoulder.

'You b . . .'

I heard it bounce to my right. I heard her run off after it.
Pitter patter bounce pitter patter bounce pitter bounce patter
bounce bounce pitter bounce bounce bounce patter bounce-
bouncebouncebouncebouncebncebncebncebncebcebcebce . . .

A car was flying up from behind.

There was this terrible braking noise.

I ran a little.

There was nothing.

Then there was running from behind me.

'You bastard! What are doing? You weirdo! I could have
been killed!'

It was alien and different. I didn't like it. It was Irish but
there was too much Englishness in there. I didn't like being
shouted at. I kept on running. I kept going. I kept going.

I was watching some show in the TV room of the hotel. The
Basque guy comes in talking some shit. He was going on
about his football team and about John Aldridge. He moves
on then to taxes to protect the ozone layer or something. I
turned around to him to tell him I was going to be settling up
that night. He said I wasn't going was I? I said I was and he
asked why.

'There's a problem in the family,' I said. 'I have to go home.'

He looked actually genuinely concerned. 'Well, all the best.
I hope everything is okay in the end.'

We went out to the desk and I paid him the cash. Things were running tight. I'd have only just been able to stay another night. Not that that influenced my decision to leave. I had my mocks to do and shit.

The security guard in the airport was a dick. Every time I'd try to settle down on the bench for a bit of sleep he'd come over. He wouldn't say anything. He'd just come over and he'd stand there. I went over to the toilets and tried to kip on a bowl, but it wasn't working. I don't think I'd have been able to sleep anyway.

6

FIFTEEN

Uncle Phil turned up really suddenly. He had that look on his face.

I asked him was everything okay. He was being a bit funny. He went on first about how it was all over between him and this African bird. I was going, 'Over?' and he went, 'Yes, over. Over, over.' He said they'd been out driving in the countryside somewhere in Nigeria and they came across this pipeline which had burst. He said the pipe was leaking oil and all the people from the surrounding villages were trying to gather up the oil in buckets. He went off in the jeep to the nearest town that had a phone to contact someone in the oil company he used to work for and he left his wife in the place with the pipeline, he said. Then someone lit a match by accident and everyone was burned to death including his wife.

There was something weird about the way he said it; I knew he was lying. He starts breaking his shites. He starts cracking up, and he goes, 'Okay, okay.' He said then that it just hadn't worked out for him with this African bird and he'd given up the thing he was doing in the British Embassy and he wanted to come back to Ireland to find a job.

He asked me how my exams went. I told him the story, about how I did my mocks, and about how I didn't do so good in them. And I told him about how I decided to drop out of school right then, and that the teachers were going, 'No, no, you can't do that, you have to do your Leaving', and I'd said, 'No I don't. I'm seventeen and I'm allowed to make these choices for myself and I could have dropped out of school after the Junior Cert, and I can leave school now if I want to.' And Uncle Phil was all right about it. He was saying it was my life and I was free to decide what to do with it. He asked me then what I was going to do now and I didn't really have an answer; I didn't really know.

So Uncle Phil just ends up staying in the house for good. I say for good, but I don't know how long it'll last. He's up in Da's room, the place we did up. It's actually okay that, because it means we never had to get any students. It would have been a nightmare, getting up, and some bird your own age seeing you in your pyjamas, or going down and having breakfast with someone who lets his cornflakes go all soggy stuck to the side of the bowl and leaving the milk stink and go yellow. Uncle Phil got some job in an office. He tried for some job in the civil service and he was looking to get this post in one of the government departments, but they turned him down so he got this job in an office.

Gary decided to go back to America for the scholarship. He'd been saying for a while that he'd intended going back over, but me and Uncle Phil were surprised with how abruptly he left. One day he'd sold his car and the next he was just . . . *gone*. He came into my room late one morning while I was still in bed and he went, 'I'm off now. See you.' I was only just coming out of sleep, and I was, 'Uuugh.' Then I woke, and I was, 'What?' and I heard him going down the stairs. I ran out and I saw him opening the door with a big rucksack and a case and I said, 'You're off? Where?' And he said that he was going to America today and the flight was at half two. Then he went out the door and he was looking down with the weight of the rucksack and he didn't look back up the stairs and the door slammed. So then it was all, 'O-*kay*. Well, bye so.'

Me and Uncle Phil were talking about it over tea a few days later. Uncle Phil asked, would I miss my brother. I said, 'I dunno', and then I could see he was embarrassed asking that sort of question and he didn't pursue it. He's not the kind of person who asks those type of questions, kind of like Da. It was as if he felt he *should* have asked it, like it was in a script, like it was in a script of some American soap opera. He could see he was being poncey, and he went silent for a minute. Then he started stroking his cheek and looking into his plate and he goes, 'I'll tell you what though. I bet there's some bird behind all this. Some bird back in America.'

We did some deadly things, me and Uncle Phil. He got me this computer somewhere and he said I could use it to my advantage. I have a couple of games for it. There's one called 'Doom' where you're underground and you're going around and you're shooting all these people. The effects are deadly. I can get pretty far in it and any day I'll have it worked out. There's this other game which I *have* completed, but I just keep going back to it because it's so mad. You start out on this level and you go along in this place like a medieval castle, except there's these things made of steel that look like pods suspended from between two legs, and they're after you. The platforms are made of wood and you go along grabbing up the 'vlorgrans' to top up your 'stamina'. There's also things called 'provisions' and 'raiment' you can collect, and special weapons. My favourite weapon is the 'blaze bolas', which wraps around the bad guys' legs, and the balls of flame meet and blow up. There are five stages of the castle, and after that you go through another four levels, each one with five stages. You go through this place made of rust, a forest, this weird place that looks like a circus with all pink colours and killer sweets, and the Hall of Osmium. Normally you can burn through walls in each of the levels with this special weapon you pick up in the first level and keep in reserve, but nothing can burn down the walls in the Hall of Osmium, because the walls there are made of this hard substance. There are different bad guys in each level, but the pods with the legs are in every level. There's this one bad guy that's made out of glass who's easy to kill but hard to see, and he can spring from anywhere and knock down your 'stamina'. The bad guy at the end is amazing. There are these challenges he sets you, like his 'minions', and the penguin thing, and a special card game, and where you have to walk across these poles, and the net you have to break down by finding the right rope, and the jump, and then you finally get to fight him. The secret is getting the box on his chest. Uncle Phil also got a modem, and a cable to put into where the phone goes in, and it's amazing. The internet just has everything. You could spend all day at it.

Another time Uncle Phil drove his car at 36 miles an hour through the wall in the front garden by accident. We had to take the whole thing down because the middle bit collapsed. He allowed me to do it with the sledgehammer. It was so deadly. There aren't many times you'd get to go at a wall with a sledgehammer. We could have just left no wall in the front garden, but I said, 'No, let's build a new one.' Uncle Phil bought all breeze blocks and cement, and while he was at work one day, I built half of it. Uncle Phil was like, 'Good man' when he came home, and over the next day I finished it off, and I kind of made it look like there were battlements going along the top. Then another day I decided to just push it over. I hadn't dug any foundations for it. I'd built it up from the ground, and one day I just decided to push it over.

Then this other time I found an old hobby horse in a skip, and I brought it back to the house. I saw this documentary about panthers on bogs in England, and I dressed the horse up in my old black bomber jacket, which I was going to throw out anyway. Then I got an indelible marker, and I went over the whole of the head until there was no white showing, and I brought the horse up to the Gaelic field and just left it there in the middle of the pitch.

Then this other time I got kicked off the *Fair City* set. I was going to this model shop in Stillorgan on the bus, and it went past RTÉ, and I looked in and I saw what was like a small town on the other side of the car park. Uncle Phil said it was where they filmed *Fair City*. I got the bus again and I got off at RTÉ, and I hid in behind this 2D house. They were setting up the recording equipment, and some people started to do a search, and this one guy with a grey bowler haircut hooshed me out with a furry microphone.

Then this other time this guy in the estate across got this MG with a fibreglass body. He made all this money really fast after he left school and he was really into cars. His name was Tom Conway and I found his number in the book. I went up

when it was dark with a Stanley knife and I lifted up the plastic
cover on the car and I scratched into the door:

TOMMY CONWAY SYSTEMS SOLUTIONS
TEL: 2965641

Then this other time I played golf with bread.

7.03

Gavin Corbett is in his twenties and studied history at Trinity College Dublin. He works as a sub-editor in a newspaper and lives in Dublin.

Bad language . 23/4 .

Newport Library & Information Service
Gwasanaeth Llyfrgell a Gwybodaeth Casnewydd

THIS ITEM SHOULD BE RETURNED OR
RENEWED BY THE LAST DATE
STAMPED BELOW

Newport
CITY COUNCIL
CYNGOR DINAS
Casnewydd

14. AUG 03   9.10.04

14 MAY 2007

0 4 JUN 2007

30 SEP 03

-1 JUL 2008

24 SEP 03   DEC 04

0 9 MAR 2009

20. MAR 06

09 OCT 03.

13. NOV   04 MAY 06

05 APR 06

01 APR 04

11. MAY 04   2 0 NOV 2006

04 OCT 04